A Dangerous Game . . .

"Dara—of all the guys you 've kissed, who was the worst kisser, and why?"

Dara let out a sharp laugh. "Hmmm . . . good question, April. The worst kisser . . ." Dara mumbled. Then slowly she raised her head and turned to the fireplace. A sly smile spread over her mouth as she gazed at Josh.

She's going to name Josh! I realized.

Josh's eyes bulged. A look of sheer panic twisted his features.

Before Dara could say another word, Josh raised the poker. "Shut up, Dara!" he screamed. "Shut up! I mean it!"

"Josh, I *have* to tell the truth," Dara declared cruelly.

"Noooo!" Josh howled.

And before any of us could move, he charged furiously at Dara, lowering the poker toward her chest.

Books by R. L. Stine

Available from ARCHWAY Paperbacks

FEAR STREET®
R·L·STINE

Truth or Dare

A Parachute Press Book

AN ARCHWAY PAPERBACK
Published by POCKET BOOKS
New York   London   Toronto   Sydney   Tokyo   Singapore

AN ARCHWAY PAPERBACK *Original*

An Archway Paperback published by
POCKET BOOKS, a division of Simon & Schuster Inc.
1230 Avenue of the Americas, New York, NY 10020

ISBN: 0-671-86836-5

First Archway Paperback printing February 1995

10 9 8 7 6 5 4 3

Cover art by David Jarvis

Printed in the U.S.A.

IL 7+

For Stuart,
World's best telephone ski instructor

Truth or Dare

chapter

1

The long, white stretch limo rolled over a deep pothole in the twisting country road. Sitting in the back, enjoying our unaccustomed luxury, my friends and I felt only the tiniest bump.

"This car is awesome!" Ken Knight declared. "I think I'll get one after graduation."

"In your dreams!" Jenny Byrd replied. "You had to borrow on your allowance to get your bike fixed!" She gave him a hard shove, which sent him bumping into me.

Jenny, Ken, and I were slouched low in the smooth, black leather seat. Ken sat in the middle. A boy named Josh Berman sat across from us.

The three of us didn't know Josh. He didn't go to Shadyside High.

Josh seemed quiet and shy. He hadn't said two words since we had stopped to pick him up.

He was short and very thin, but kind of good looking. He had wavy black hair and dark eyes. He wore glasses and kept constantly pushing them up on his nose. A nervous habit.

As we rode along, he stared out the window, pretending to be interested in the scenery. Sometimes he laughed at the things we said. But he didn't offer comments of his own.

Too shy, I guessed.

"April, I'll buy you a limo, too," Ken declared, turning to me with a grin. "What color do you want?"

"Lime green," I answered without thinking about it. "And I'd like a sky blue one, too. For weekends. With a pale blond interior—to match my hair."

"Okay. One lime green limo for Ms. April Leeds," Ken said. "If Dara can have a limo, I don't see why we can't all have one."

"Dara is rich," I reminded Ken, even though I didn't have to. We all knew that Dara Harker was rich. Dara reminded us constantly.

"Where is Dara?" Josh suddenly spoke up. He had been silent for so long, he startled me. "She told me she'd be riding to the ski house with us," he said.

"Huh? Are you kidding? Dara ride with us peasants?" Ken cried in mock horror.

Jenny and I laughed. But Josh didn't crack a smile.

2

"Dara is coming up with her parents in the Jeep," I told him. "So we'll have a four-wheel drive car in the snow."

"What snow?" Jenny complained, glancing out the window.

Evening had fallen, sending a hazy wash of gray over the passing farms. A silvery frost blanketed the dark, winter-bare fields. It was cold enough to snow. But we hadn't seen a single flake in days.

"I turned on The Weather Channel before I left," Jenny said, brushing back her short brown hair. She tugged down the sleeves of her sweater. "I always watch The Weather Channel before I go anywhere. They said a forty-percent chance—"

"Of flurries. Maybe sleet instead of snow," Ken said.

I groaned. Jenny and Ken have been going together for so long, they finish each other's sentences. It's really disgusting. Sometimes they're like an old married couple.

They even fight like an old married couple. They yell at each other and call each other all kinds of horrible names. Then they kiss and make up and act as if nothing happened.

I've seen them do it. And even though Jenny is my best friend, I have to say it—it's disgusting.

Maybe I'm jealous. I don't know.

I guess I'm jealous of Jenny's dark, dramatic good looks. She's just about the most beautiful girl at Shadyside High, in my opinion. She has perfect hair, short and dark brown and sleek. And perfect, oval-shaped, blue eyes. And beautiful skin that always looks tanned.

Jenny had a good bod, too. Not skinny and shapeless like mine. My little brother Jerry says I look like a ten-year-old boy.

Nice kid, huh?

With those awesome looks, Jenny should be the most confident person in the world. But she gets nervous at parties and sometimes gets totally tongue-tied in class. And she clings to Ken as if she can't get along without him.

I don't know *what* her problem is. Not that Ken isn't good enough for her. He treats Jenny pretty nicely, actually. So many girls would die to go out with Ken. He's probably one of the best-looking guys at school, with his thick wavy dark hair and dark eyes. And he's definitely the best built—tall and muscular, but not too bulky.

"What kind of Jeep does Dara have?" Jenny asked. "A Renegade?"

"No way," Ken replied, shaking his head. "She's *got* to have a Grand Cherokee. It's the biggest Jeep they make. It's like a truck!"

"If it doesn't snow, we'll die of boredom!" I declared unhappily.

"Maybe you will. But *we* won't!" Ken replied, snickering. He turned and nuzzled his face against Jenny's cheek. She kissed him.

Why do I have to spend so much time in my life watching Jenny and Ken make out?

I turned my attention to Josh. "Where do you go to school?" I asked.

He cleared his throat and pushed his glasses up on his nose. "Cumberland," he replied.

He wore a dark ski sweater over baggy, faded jeans. He had his hands shoved into his jeans pockets.

"What year?" I asked.

"Eleventh grade," he said.

"Me, too. How do you know Dara?" I asked.

"My father works with her father," Josh replied, glancing out the window. "They're partners in the same law firm. Sometimes we vacation together. Up at Cape Cod. I've been kind of bored. So I asked Dara if I could come up this weekend."

"So you know Dara pretty well," I commented.

"Yeah. Pretty well," he said. I thought I saw his cheeks turn red.

He turned to the window again, and I saw a glint of silver. A tiny lightning bolt in one earlobe.

We rode along in silence for a minute or so. It was hard to keep a conversation going with Josh. I was running out of questions.

Why did I have to ask all the questions? I wondered. Why didn't Josh ask *me* something?

"We don't know Dara that well," I babbled on. "I mean, Dara hasn't lived in Shadyside long. We sit next to each other in science lab. And Dara asked if I'd like to come skiing this weekend and see her fabulous ski house. She said I could invite Ken and Jenny. So, here we are."

Josh nodded but didn't reply.

He was really giving me a pain. I don't like the strong, silent types. Or the *weak,* silent types. I decided to *force* him to talk.

"Do you ski?" I asked.

"I ski a little. Just well enough to break some bones!" he replied.

We both laughed. I was glad to see that at least Josh had a sense of humor.

The fields had given way to pine woods, and the limo started to climb steep hills. We all took Cokes from the little refrigerator. Jenny picked up the car phone. She called our friend Corky Corcoran back in Shadyside and bragged about how she was calling from a limo.

"Who else can we call?" Ken asked.

But the limo stopped suddenly. Ken set the phone back on its holder. The driver climbed out and opened the back door for us.

"Hey—we're here!" I declared.

I slid out onto the gravel driveway in front of the garage and took a deep breath. Cool, fresh mountain air.

I shivered. It was much colder up here than it had been back in Shadyside. I gazed around at the dark pines that covered the hills, black shadows against a starless, purple night sky.

"Hey—was that a snowflake?" Ken asked, holding both palms up.

"You're the only flake up here!" Jenny teased him. She shoved him with both hands.

He pretended to stagger back until he landed on the hood of the limo. The driver had moved to the trunk and was pulling out our bags and our skis.

I turned and gazed at Dara's house. "Wow!" I uttered out loud. The house was long and low—and beautiful.

Jenny and Ken stepped up beside me, their shoes crunching over the gravel. "It's so much bigger than I expected!" I exclaimed.

Built of redwood panels, with enormous windows along the front, the house looked like a traditional ski lodge—a ski lodge that had been stretched out to cover the entire hilltop.

"I've been here before," Josh announced. "It's awesome. There are no other houses around to ruin the view. There are glass doors and huge windows in back. You can see down the hill for miles!"

Pale white light suddenly rolled over the front of the house. We turned and saw two headlights floating through the darkness, hovering nearer.

Dara's Jeep pulled up beside the limo, jerking to an abrupt stop an inch or two from our suitcases. The headlights flared over the front of the house.

Dara honked the horn twice. Then she jumped out and came running over to greet us, her streaky blond hair flying behind her.

She was alone, I saw. No parents.

"You got here so fast!" she cried. "I wanted to be here before you arrived." Dara's blue ski jacket was unzipped over a white sweater.

"Dara, where are your parents?" I asked.

"They couldn't make it. But I'm sure we can survive without them!" Dara declared with a mischievous gleam in her eyes.

I swallowed hard. I knew my parents would never approve. But I was here now. I decided I just wouldn't tell them.

"Where's the snow?" she demanded, gazing up at the sky. "How can we ski without snow? We'll go crazy up here. What will we do? I *hate* charades. Promise me we won't play charades. And I stink at Trivial Pursuit. I can't remember anything about *The Partridge Family* or *The Brady Bunch*. Really. The last time I played, I threw the cards in the fire."

That's the way Dara always talks. Without taking a breath. Always excited. And she has a hoarse, croaky kind of voice, which makes her sound kind of comical.

Dara is nice looking, really cute, but not naturally beautiful like Jenny. She has long tangles of crimped, blond hair which she has streaked with white-blond. She has a perky little nose. I don't think it's hers. I think she had a nose job before she moved to Shadyside last year.

Her best feature is her eyes. They're big and round and pale, pale blue.

Dara fumbled in a pocket of her ski jacket and pulled out her keys. "It's *got* to snow. Maybe we'll all do a snow dance under the moonlight later," she said as she unlocked the front door and pushed it open.

She turned to the limo driver. "Frank, would you

bring the bags into the house? I'll show you where they go. The skis go in the locker around back."

The driver nodded and moved quickly to grab up the bags.

"Hi, Dara." Josh stepped forward shyly, his hands awkwardly at his sides.

"Oh. Josh. I didn't see you!" Dara exclaimed. "I forgot you were coming," she added cruelly. "Hey, listen. Invite yourself up anytime. You know there's plenty of room. How's it going?"

She didn't wait for Josh to reply. Instead, she turned to me. "April, let me see that parka. Does it have a fur lining? I've been looking for one just like that."

I caught a hurt expression on Josh's face. I think he hoped for a better greeting from Dara.

I was holding my new blue ski parka in my arms. I held it up for Dara to see it. "It's really warm," I said, "and it wasn't very expensive."

I suddenly felt foolish. Dara didn't care if the parka was expensive or not. Her family didn't have to pinch pennies like mine. She probably didn't even check out the price tag when she bought a coat.

"What's the fur inside?" she asked, rubbing it with her palm. "Mmmmm. Soft."

"I think it's *dog* fur!" I joked. And then I added, "Actually, it's fake."

Dara laughed. "Come on in, guys." She held open the storm door. "I hope the heat is on. The furnace conked out last winter, and all the pipes froze. Just be thankful you weren't here. My dad went ballistic!"

I followed Ken and Jenny into the house. Behind

me, I heard Josh say something to Dara. But she didn't hear him. She was giving Frank, the driver, more instructions.

It was pitch black inside the house. I fumbled on the wall for the light switch, but couldn't find it.

I heard the limo door slam. Headlights slid over the wall as the car backed down the drive. Frank was driving the limo back the hundred miles to Shadyside.

Josh moved beside me. Just ahead of us, Ken had his arm around Jenny's shoulders.

"Dara—where's the light?" I called. I took a step forward. It was so dark!

"Hey—!" Jenny let out a low cry of surprise. "What was that?" she whispered.

I heard it, too. A creaking floorboard.

All four of us froze in the darkness, listening hard.

I heard a footstep.

Then a *thud,* the sound of someone bumping against a chair or table.

A cough.

We're not alone, I realized. *Someone is in here with us.*

chapter

2

I took a step back.

The footsteps came closer. I heard another cough.

Behind me, Dara was just entering the house. She hadn't heard the sounds yet.

Who was in the house? I wondered, gripped with fear. Some homeless people who had wandered in during the week?

Burglars?

The lights clicked on.

"Hey—!" Dara cried in surprise.

We stared at a boy and a girl, about our age.

They stared back at us. They appeared just as startled as we were.

"Tony—what are *you* doing here?" Dara demanded. She knew the guy. Her tone wasn't exactly warm.

"Dara—I . . . uh . . . well . . ." he stammered. As he stepped forward, I could see that his long, brown hair was messed up, and he had smeared purple lipstick marks all over his cheeks and chin.

I didn't have to guess that Tony and the girl had been making out in the dark. They were so involved with each other they hadn't heard us drive up.

"Uh . . . hi, Dara," Tony said.

He had a nice smile. But I didn't really like his face. There was something smug and stuck-up about it. I could see that right away.

And I hate guys with deep clefts in their chins. I don't know why. I just don't like it.

"This is Carly Rae," Tony told Dara. He pulled the girl forward.

She seemed really embarrassed. "Nice to meet you," she muttered. Carly's purple lipstick was smeared. And her auburn hair was messed up, too, down over her forehead. She sure had a lot of it!

She was short and skinny. She wore a red sweater that really didn't look good with her hair color. She had on a short black skirt over red tights. Her gums showed when she smiled.

"This isn't your week," Dara told him angrily, hands pressed against her waist. "I can't believe you—you—"

Tony slapped his forehead. "Did I mess up?"

Carly wiped a purple lipstick smear off Tony's cheek with one hand.

"Did I mess up?" Tony repeated. "I'm sorry, Dara. I really thought this was my family's week!"

He didn't sound very sincere. I had never seen him before, but I could tell he was putting on a performance. He seemed like a pretty phony guy.

Dara turned to Jenny, Ken, and me. "Meet Tony Macedo. His family and my family share this house," she explained. "We have it every other week."

"And I thought it was our week!" Tony declared, shaking his head.

"It's a really nice house," Carly commented to Dara. "Very pretty."

How could you see any of it in the dark? I wondered.

"Tony, I don't believe you did this!" Dara said sharply, ignoring Carly's compliment. Dara blew a wisp of hair off her forehead. I could see she was really angry.

Tony's mouth spread into a sheepish grin. "I don't believe I did it, either," he replied.

He slid an arm around Carly's waist. She cuddled against him and mumbled something in his ear. They couldn't seem to keep their hands off each other.

"But—I don't get it!" Dara sputtered. "Don't your parents keep a calendar? Don't they keep a record of—"

"My parents don't actually know I'm here," Tony confessed. His dark eyes flashed. "You can keep a secret—right, Dara?" He tried to keep it light. But

I thought I heard a tiny threat in the way Tony said it.

"I mean, Carly and I sort of decided to come here at the last minute," he added.

Carly smiled her toothy smile at us and held on to Tony.

"But how did you get here?" Dara demanded. "I didn't see a car or anything outside."

"We flew up to Eastham," Carly answered. "Then we took a taxi."

"You came all the way up here without a car?" Dara rolled her eyes.

"We really didn't think about it," Tony replied. "It was a tough week. We just wanted to get away. You know. Do some skiing."

I wondered if they had brought skis. They didn't seem to have *outdoor* activities on their minds at all!

Suddenly Dara leaned close to me. "He's trouble," she whispered. "Tony is always trouble."

What did she mean? I wondered. I didn't have a chance to ask.

Tossing her streaked hair over her shoulder, Dara turned back to Tony. "Well, how are we going to settle this?" she demanded.

"Settle it?" He pretended he didn't understand.

I didn't really understand what she meant, either.

"Who's staying and who's going?" Dara asked sharply.

Tony's smile faded. His dark eyes narrowed menacingly.

I felt a chill of fear. *He can be dangerous,* I found myself thinking.

He let go of Carly and took a step toward Dara. His expression hardened. He balled both hands into fists.

He's deliberately trying to scare us, I realized.

"*I* know how to settle it," Tony said coldly.

chapter

—————
3

Dara didn't back down. She kept her hands pressed against her waist and stood her ground.

Tony took another menacing step toward her.

Ken stepped up beside Dara and glared at Tony.

Ken is bigger than Tony, I thought. And a lot more powerful looking. If there is a fight, I think Ken would win.

"Only one way to settle it," Tony repeated. "We'll just have to share!" He burst out laughing.

I let out a sigh of relief. Tony had really fooled me.

Dara shook her head and frowned. "Tony, you

really are a jerk," she muttered. "Did I ever tell you how much I hate your sick sense of humor?"

"Lots of times," Tony replied. "But at least I *have* a sense of humor, Dara!"

"Ooh. Good one!" Josh chimed in.

I had completely forgotten Josh was there. He had wandered over by the fireplace, across the room from the rest of us. He had lifted a fireplace poker from its stand and held it in one hand.

"You keep out of it, Josh," Dara said sharply.

"Yeah. Keep out of it, Josh," Tony parroted, grinning. He turned to Dara. "Who's Josh?"

"Just a guy," Dara replied. "His father and my father work together."

"Hmmm. Lawyer dudes!" Tony exclaimed.

Dara introduced the rest of us to Tony and Carly. Tony spent a long time gazing at Jenny, checking her out. I caught an annoyed glimmer in Carly's eyes. She wrapped her hands around Tony's arm.

"I guess we have no choice. We'll share the house," Dara agreed grudgingly. She gazed sternly at Tony. "I guess we can get along for one weekend."

"There's a first time for everything!" he declared.

Carly laughed uncomfortably.

Jenny and I exchanged glances. It was obvious to both of us that Dara had had trouble with Tony in the past.

"There are plenty of bedrooms," Dara said, counting them on her fingers. She stared up at Tony, who was nuzzling Carly's cheek. "Do you and Carly plan to share a room?"

Tony stepped away from Carly. He shook his head at Dara. "You always did have a dirty mind," he told her.

"It takes one to know one!" Dara shot back.

"Carly and I have already staked out separate rooms," Tony replied, ignoring Dara's wisecrack. He gestured to Ken and Josh. "Those guys can share the room with the bunk bed. No problem."

"I have to sleep on the top," Josh said, swinging the fireplace poker. "I get claustrophobic."

"No problem," Ken replied.

"See? And all the girls get to have their very own rooms," Tony said, grinning his smug grin. He walked over and draped an arm around Dara's shoulders. "Isn't this going to be fun?"

Dara glared back at him coldly and didn't reply.

We all went to our rooms to unpack. The house stretched out in two long wings, with the big living room and the kitchen in the middle. The boys' rooms were down at the end of the long hall that stretched to the left.

The girls took the wing to the right. Dara had her own room, the one nearest the living room. Jenny and I had rooms across from each other, halfway down the hall. Carly's room was next to Jenny's.

Jenny unpacked quickly and came into my room. "What a view!" she declared, pulling back the white curtains and peering out the double glass doors.

I stepped up beside her. We could see dark pine

trees all the way down the steeply sloping hill. The night sky had turned a hazy pink.

"Look—it's snowing!" I cried, pointing.

"Call that snow?" Jenny complained. "It's just a few flakes."

"But it's a start!" I declared cheerily.

I really wanted to have a good time this weekend. It had been a pretty dreary winter for me so far. I had broken up with my boyfriend in October. A few weeks after that, my mom had lost her job, which meant the family was on an even tighter budget than usual. And then I had missed nearly two weeks of school with a really bad flu.

Time to have some fun, I decided.

As I told Josh in the car, I didn't know Dara very well. She had moved to Shadyside a few weeks before school started. But when she invited me to her ski house, I jumped at the chance.

Jenny and I returned to the living room to find a bright fire blazing in the wide stone fireplace. Ken and Tony were piling on more logs from a basket of firewood in the corner.

I was glad they had built the fire. With all the big windows and sliding glass doors, the house was really drafty. As I lowered myself into a soft, comfortable armchair facing the fire, I could feel the chill of a breeze from the glass doors behind me.

Feeling the warmth of the fire, listening to it crackle, I gazed around the big, wood-paneled room. There were two seating areas, two circles of armchairs and dark leather couches. A long, wooden coffee table was cluttered with stacks of old magazines and newspapers. Large, framed posters of European ski resorts filled the walls.

Tony stepped away from the fire and turned to admire it for a few seconds. Then he joined Carly on a couch at the back of the room.

A few seconds later the two of them were smooching away. They didn't seem to care—or even notice—that the rest of us were there in the room!

Ken and Jenny shared a big, overstuffed armchair near me. They gazed silently at the fire. Josh sat by himself on the end of the couch, tapping his hand rapidly on the padded arm.

"Come on, snow!" Dara cried. She stood at the window, her hands pressed against the glass, peering out at the few flakes drifting slowly down from the sky.

"What does a pink sky mean?" she demanded. "Does that mean snow or no snow?"

"It means pink snow!" Ken joked.

Dara spun around and rolled her eyes. "You're about as funny as Tony," she told Ken. Then she turned to the couple in the back of the room. "Don't you two ever come up for air?"

"We don't hear you," Tony called back to her.

Dara dropped down on the other end of Josh's couch. "Nice fire," she commented, raising her feet to the coffee table. "We'll have to get more firewood later."

The five of us chatted for a while. About school. And about kids we knew.

I kept glancing over at the front window, checking out the snow. It was coming down a little harder, big, fluffy flakes.

"I know a great way to start a weekend," Ken said suddenly, scratching his thick brown hair.

"A big snowfall would start the weekend off just right," Dara commented.

"No. I mean, break the ice," Ken said. "We don't really know each other that well." He glanced at Josh, who had stopped tapping his hand and was staring into the fire. "It would be fun to play a game or something. Something to help us get to know one another. Truth or Dare!"

"Excuse me? I don't think so!" Josh declared.

"Don't you like to play Truth or Dare?" I asked him.

Josh shook his head. "I don't really like games." He glanced uncomfortably at Dara.

"I think it's a *great* idea!" Dara exclaimed excitedly. "Let's do it! Let's play. It's a perfect game for tonight. Let's see what dirty secrets we can drag out of one another."

I laughed. I found myself beginning to like Dara. I liked the way she threw herself into things, the way she got excited so quickly.

Dara lowered her feet and leaned forward eagerly. We all leaned forward. Josh groaned, but agreed to join us.

21

And so we began our game of Truth or Dare.

It seemed like a really good idea at the time.

As Ken had said, a good way to break the ice, to get to know one another.

We had no way of knowing that a simple game would lead us to so much horror.

chapter

4

"*T*ony, do you two want to play?" Dara called to the back of the room.

They didn't reply.

Something popped in the fire. The sound made me jump. I realized I felt a little tense.

I always get tense before starting a game like this. I guess everyone does. I mean, it's so easy to make a total fool of yourself in Truth or Dare.

"I've never played Truth or Dare," Josh confessed. He pushed back his black hair, then adjusted his glasses. "Is it like Twenty Questions?"

"No way," Jenny replied.

"Truth or Dare is real simple," Dara told Josh. "Even *you* can get it."

"Oh, wow. You're cruel tonight, Dara," Josh accused, shaking his head.

"Just being a good hostess," Dara joked.

"Either you answer a question with the truth, or you accept a dare," Ken explained to Josh. "That's all there is to it."

Josh still appeared puzzled.

"You'll see how it works," Dara told him. "Ken can take the first question—since this was his idea."

"Uh-oh!" Ken gulped. He glanced at Jenny, who snuggled beside him in the big armchair.

The flickering, darting fire made shadows dance over the room. Outside, I could see the snow starting to come down harder. I smiled, feeling warm and cozy in front of the fire.

"What is something you did that you're really ashamed of?" Dara asked Ken.

"Excuse me?" he cried, his mouth dropping open.

Dara asked it again. "What is something that bothered your conscience for a long, long time?"

Ken laughed. "Oh, wow. I think Josh should go first. Since it's his first game."

"No way!" Josh cried. He jumped up from the couch and made his way to the fireplace.

"Just kidding," Ken told him.

"Will you answer the question?" Dara asked Ken. "Or will you take a dare?"

"Uh . . . don't you have any multiple-choice questions?" Ken joked.

"Hey, Ken—this was *your* idea!" I shouted. "Come on—let's play!"

"Okay, okay," he grumbled, shifting uncomfortably in the chair. "I'll answer the question."

Josh picked up the fireplace poker and began poking at the logs, sending up glowing cinders.

"Uh . . . something I'm ashamed of," Ken murmured, thinking hard.

"You'd better leave *me* out of it!" Jenny threatened. She laughed an uncomfortable laugh.

"Oh. I remember something," Ken told us. "This was pretty bad."

"It'd better be!" Dara said.

"I was in a store once, a long time ago. It was that comic book store on Division Street. Remember it? I don't think it's there anymore."

"This is boring," Josh muttered, poking at the fire.

"Ssshhh. Let him get to the good part," Dara told Josh.

"Well," Ken continued, "I saw a kid in there. A little kid, maybe seven or eight. And the kid dropped a ten-dollar bill. I guess it fell out of his pocket. And I—I picked it up off the floor and jammed it in my pocket. The kid searched and searched for it. And he started to cry. But I didn't tell him I'd found it. I kept the ten dollars."

"And what did you do with it?" Dara asked him.

"Bought comic books," Ken replied. "Pretty bad, huh? It bothered me for months!"

"Ken—I don't believe you! That's the *worst* thing you ever did?" Jenny exclaimed, shaking her head.

A grin spread over Ken's face. "What can I tell you? Normally, I'm a saint!" he boasted.

"Bor-ring!" Dara declared.

"You asked for something that stayed on my conscience!" Ken cried. "So—I answered the question!"

"But we want something sexy!" Dara complained. "We don't want to hear a dumb story about finding ten dollars in a comic book store."

"Ken thinks ten dollars *is* sexy!" I joked.

Everybody laughed.

"Let's think of a sexy question for Dara," Ken suggested.

"Whoa!" Dara held up both hands as if to shield herself. A grin spread over her face. "I've got a sexy question for you, April."

"Uh-oh," I murmured. I swallowed hard.

Dara's eyes gleamed with excitement. "What's the most embarrassing thing that ever happened to you while you were making out with a boy?" she asked me.

"You mean, like, did I burp or something?" I asked, thinking hard. I could feel my face turn red hot. I knew I was blushing.

"The question or the dare?" Dara insisted.

"Uh . . . the question," I answered. "Once I was down in our family room kissing this boy—"

"Who?" Ken demanded, grinning.

"Yeah. Who?" Tony chimed in from the back of the room.

"You wouldn't know him," I called back to him. "Anyway, I was kissing him, and I forgot I was chewing gum. And somehow my gum went from my mouth into his."

"Ooh, gross!" Jenny declared, making a disgusted face.

"And he started to choke on it," I added. "And I had to keep slapping him on the back until he coughed it up."

"Yuck!" Jenny murmured.

"Pretty good," Dara commented.

My face was still red hot. I *hate* embarrassing games like this. At least my turn is over for now, I thought gratefully.

An idea popped into my head. "Dara, I have a kissing question for you."

"I'm listening," she said, resting her chin in her hand and staring hard at me.

"Dara—of all the guys you've kissed, who was the worst kisser, and why?"

Dara let out a sharp laugh. "Hmmm . . . good question, April."

Jenny giggled.

Ken eyed her sternly. "Jenny, it's Dara's question. What are *you* giggling about?"

"The question or the dare?" I asked Dara.

"The question," she replied quickly. "The worst kisser, huh?"

Slowly she raised her head and turned to the fireplace. A sly smile spread over her face as she gazed at Josh.

She's going to name Josh! I realized.

Josh's eyes bulged. A look of sheer panic twisted his features.

Dara wouldn't do that, I told myself. She couldn't be that mean—could she?

Her mischievous smile grew wider as she locked her eyes on Josh. "Hmmm . . . the worst kisser . . ."

Before Dara could say another word, Josh raised the poker. "Shut up, Dara!" he screamed. "Shut up! I mean it!"

"Josh, I *have* to tell the truth!" Dara declared cruelly.

"Noooo!" Josh uttered a raging howl.

And before any of us could move, he came charging furiously at Dara, lowering the poker toward her chest.

chapter

5

Dara let out a frightened shriek. She shot out her hands as if to shield herself.

Josh stopped inches in front of her, breathing hard. He heaved the poker to the floor. And with a furious cry he spun around and ran to the hallway door leading to the left wing.

"Josh—stop!" Dara cried. She leaped to her feet and took off after him.

My heart pounding, I stood up and turned to the doorway. Jenny and Ken were on their feet, too. Even Tony and Carla gaped in shock.

"What's his problem?" Jenny whispered to me.

I shrugged. I was as startled as everyone else.

Dara caught up with Josh at the door. She threw her arms around his neck and dragged him back toward the fire.

"Come on back, Josh. Come on," she pleaded. "Did you really think I was going to name you? Did you? I was teasing. You know me, Josh. I guess I have a mean streak or something. I wasn't going to name you. I was just trying to get a reaction. That's all."

She kept talking to him, soothing him, pulling him back. "Josh—come on!"

He stopped trying to escape. Now he just stood there, eyes on the floor, a very unhappy expression on his face.

I thought he might burst into tears. He looked so sad and forlorn.

Dara stopped halfway across the room, stepped around him, and pressed her forehead against his. "Sorry," she said. "Sorry, Josh."

She let go of him and stepped back. "Apology accepted?"

"I guess," Josh muttered. Even from across the room, I could see that his face was bright red.

Josh fiddled nervously with his glasses. "Don't make fun of me," he told Dara sternly, turning his eyes to the window. "I don't like to be made fun of. I really don't."

"Okay, okay," Dara replied softly. She pulled Josh back to the couch and then sat down.

"Can't you play a quieter game?" Tony chimed in

from the back of the room. "How about tackle football? That would be quieter."

"Ha, ha," Dara called back to Tony. "You're so funny, Tony. Wish I could be as funny as you are."

"You are funny!" Tony shot back. "Funny looking." He let out a high-pitched hyena laugh.

"Shut up, Tony," I heard Carly scold him in a whisper.

"Who's going to make me?" Tony demanded loudly.

He really thought he was a riot.

"Can we get something to drink?" I heard Carly ask. I think she was just trying to get Tony to be quiet.

"Yeah, sure," Tony replied. They got up and made their way into the kitchen.

"Ignore them," Dara urged, turning back to us. She slid closer to Josh on the couch and smiled at him. "Let's go on with the game, okay?"

Josh shrugged. He was still steaming, I think.

Why was he so angry? I wondered. Or was he just hurt that Dara was going to tell us he was a terrible kisser?

What had gone on between Dara and Josh in the past? If Dara had gone with Josh and broke up with him, why did she let him come for the weekend?

Questions. Questions.

"I've got another question for April," Dara said, staring at me thoughtfully.

"Hey, no way!" I protested. "I've already had a question. And besides, you didn't answer *your* question."

"I'm the host," Dara replied smugly. "I get to make the rules. I've got a good question for you, April."

"Oh, good," Jenny said eagerly. She leaned forward. "April is always so private. I'd love to hear her tell a deep, dark secret."

Jenny's words surprised me. I never really think of myself as a private person.

But Jenny is my best friend. She knows me better than anyone else. Maybe I *am* kind of private, I found myself thinking. Maybe I do keep too much inside.

"Here's my second question for you," Dara said, sweeping back her masses of hair. "April, what secret do you know about someone that you wish you didn't know?"

I took a deep breath. And then without stopping for a second to think, I answered, "I wish I didn't know about the girl on Sumner Island."

"What girl?" Jenny demanded. "April—what are you talking about?"

I immediately regretted saying it.

Why had I blurted out that answer? Why hadn't I thought about it first? Why hadn't I stopped myself?

If only I could take the answer back.

But it was too late.

Feeling my face go red, I glanced at Ken. Did he realize that it was *his* secret—and that I knew it?

He stared straight ahead at the fire. But I could see his eyes narrow. I could see that he was thinking hard about what I had just revealed.

"What girl do you mean?" Jenny asked again.

Before I could answer, Tony crept up behind me and slapped the back of my chair. I let out a shriek and practically jumped out of my skin.

He let out a long burst of hooting laughter.

"Tony, you really are a jerk," Dara said, shaking her head.

"Takes one to know one," he shot back. He eased down beside me in the chair. "I like you, April," he said, sliding his arm around my shoulders. "You're my type."

I turned uncomfortably and saw Carly rolling her eyes. I guess she was used to Tony's dumb flirting games.

"I have a question for you, Tony," Dara said teasingly. "I know you have a lot of dirty secrets."

"Almost as many as you, Dara," he said, grinning back at her. "But, tell you what—skip the question. I'll take the dare."

We all laughed.

"I'm serious," Tony insisted, staring at Dara. "I'll take a dare. Any dare."

"What a macho guy," Dara replied sarcastically.

"Tony, you're really crazy," Carly muttered.

"I've got a perfect dare for you," Dara told him. She jumped to her feet. "Come on, everyone. Get your coats."

We followed her to the front. I peered through the sliding glass door. "Wow! Look at the snow!" I cried excitedly.

"It's really coming down now," Jenny said, beside me. "It'll be great skiing by tomorrow."

We pulled on our coats and scarves and gloves. Then we hurried outside.

Dara stopped on the driveway. She turned back to the house and pointed up to the slanting roof. "There's your dare. Up there, Tony."

Squinting through the falling snow, I could make out a dark, round object on the shingles.

"What are you talking about?" Tony demanded, stepping up close to Dara.

"That Frisbee up on the roof. You threw it up there—didn't you?" Dara said.

Tony shrugged. "So?"

"So climb up and bring it down," Dara instructed. "I dare you."

"But it's real slippery up there," Carly protested, her auburn hair fluttering around her face. "And the snow is already sticking."

"Hey—no problem," Tony said. "That's too easy, Dara."

"Don't do it, Tony," I blurted out. "Carly is right. The snow will make it real slick up there. It's too dangerous."

Dara narrowed her eyes at me, as if to say, "Butt out."

"I'll take that dare," Tony said. He started toward the garage. Halfway there, he turned back to us. "If I fall off, I know you won't feel too guilty or anything—will you, Dara?"

"Don't make me laugh. I have chapped lips," Dara replied nastily.

A few seconds later Tony emerged from the garage

with an aluminum ladder. He propped it up against the front of the house. He turned to take a deep bow before starting up the ladder.

The wind picked up suddenly, swirling the snow in circles. I shivered. A heavy feeling of dread rose from my stomach.

He shouldn't be doing this, I thought, wiping snowflakes off my eyebrows. This is crazy.

Dara doesn't like Tony, and she's really being mean to him.

And he's too big a show-off to back down.

I closed my eyes as Tony stepped onto the slanting roof. But I couldn't keep them closed. I had to watch.

I huddled close to Jenny and Ken. Josh stood by himself in the driveway, hands shoved in his pockets. Snowflakes had spotted his glasses. Dara stood closest to the house, her arms crossed, an unpleasant smirk on her face.

"Hey, it's great up here!" Tony cried, taking a step toward the Frisbee, then another. "You should all try it!"

He leaned forward, ducking against the swirling wind. He took a step. His foot slid. He caught his balance.

"Tony—come down!" Carly pleaded. "Come *on!* You've proved you're a macho guy. Come down—okay?"

He ignored her. Took another step across the snowy roof. Reached down for the Frisbee.

I let out a loud gasp as I saw his feet slide. Both feet. Slipping out from under him.

His hands shot forward.

He uttered a startled cry.

The front of his coat hit the roof hard. His arms and legs thrashed wildly.

We all screamed as he slid down the roof.

chapter
6

*T*ony's hands scraped against the shingles as he fell.

He slid fast—too fast for any of us to move.

His legs dangled over the edge, kicking frantically.

And then he caught the gutter with both hands.

And held on.

"Tony—!" Carly shrieked. "Tony—!"

He hung from the gutter for a moment—his feet swinging high above the snow. Then in one quick motion, Tony released his grip and leaped safely to the ground.

I let out a long sigh of relief. Everyone cheered and clapped.

A wide grin on his face, Tony came jogging across

the snowy front lawn. He put an arm around Carly's shoulders and turned to Dara.

Dara pointed to the roof. "You forgot the Frisbee," she said.

We all laughed.

But Tony glared coldly back at her. "Get it yourself," he muttered. "I'm out of the game."

They really don't like each other, I realized. I wondered if they'd be able to spend this long weekend together without spoiling it for everyone.

"Let's take a walk!" I suggested. "It's so beautiful out! Let's walk in the woods."

Dara's house stood at the top of the hill. Below it stretched dark pine woods. The ski slopes started about half a mile past the woods. The nearest town stood about a mile past the ski slopes.

I pulled up the hood of my parka and led the way down the sloping, snow-covered hill toward the woods. Everyone began laughing and singing. Even Tony joined in.

We spun around wildly, bumping into and pulling at each other, raising our faces to the wet snow. The sky was a dark purple. The snow came down so hard and thick, I could barely see the trees.

"I can't see a thing!" Josh complained. His glasses were completely covered by snowflakes.

As we entered the woods, we could see the snow clinging to the tree limbs. So beautiful. It looked like a Christmas card.

I lingered behind. I kept thinking about my answer in the Truth or Dare game.

I tried to forget about it. But my words followed me outside, stayed with me, repeating, filling me with dread as I tried to enjoy the beautiful night.

Sumner Island.

Since last summer I couldn't get it out of my mind. Couldn't stop thinking about what I saw there.

And every time I thought about it, I felt more and more guilty.

chapter

7

*T*hat hot, steamy August. A heat wave. Hardly a breeze.

I was working as a mother's helper. Sumner Island was so pretty, so quaint. With its white, clapboard cottages, its carefully tended flower beds, the narrow beaches of white sand, the small, wooden docks bobbing in the smooth, sparkling water.

I was having a nice vacation. A little boring maybe. But nice. Soaking up the sun. Swimming. Reading. Hanging out with some friends in the little two-block town after dark.

It was all ruined when I saw Ken.

I knew Ken and his family were vacationing on

Sumner Island. But I hadn't run into him during my first week there.

Then I saw him on the beach. With a girl I didn't recognize. With a girl that wasn't Jenny.

She was very tanned. I think I noticed her tan before I noticed anything else. She had short black hair, sort of bobbed, with bangs.

I didn't see her face clearly. I was standing on the rocks at the edge of the beach. Too shocked to go any closer.

She wore a tiny blue bikini. I remember that.

She and Ken had spread two big beach towels on the sand. But they both lay on only one of them. All tangled in each other.

Ken was kissing her. A long kiss.

They didn't move.

I didn't move, either. I stood gaping at them. I was so shocked. Totally stunned.

Finally I turned and ran from the beach. I glanced back once. Ken and the girl hadn't moved. They were still kissing.

I saw them in town the next day, but they didn't see me. Ken had his arm draped around her shoulders. They stopped in the middle of the town square to kiss.

I never told Jenny. I knew she would be crushed.

I never told Ken that I had seen him. That I knew he had spent his vacation with another girl.

I felt so guilty.

I knew this terrible secret about Ken. But I just couldn't bring myself to tell Jenny. I didn't want to hurt her.

After the vacation she and Ken were back together as always. I wanted to tell Jenny what I had seen. I wanted to tell her that Ken wasn't the guy she thought he was.

I felt so guilty for keeping this secret from my best friend.

But I didn't have the nerve to tell her.

A couple of times I started to tell her. I dialed her number—but then I hung up.

As the months passed, I thought maybe I could forget about it. Forget about what I saw on Sumner Island.

But I couldn't stop thinking about it. I felt more and more guilty.

I guess that's why I blurted out that answer in the Truth or Dare game. I've been dying to let the secret out. It really is a secret I wish I didn't know.

The words burst out of me. I didn't really think.

And then I felt so bad that I had said them.

I wondered if Ken knew what I was talking about.

He *must* know, I decided. Now, for the first time, Ken must know that I know.

"Hey, April—what are you doing back there?" Jenny called from up ahead.

Brushing snow out of my eyes, I hurried to catch up.

We tossed our wet coats in a pile in the front entryway. The fire had died down to a dark glow on the fireplace floor. But steaming mugs of hot chocolate warmed us up.

The long walk through the woods had helped to ease the tense mood. Carly and Tony were laughing and joking with the rest of us.

Even Josh seemed to be getting over his shyness. Although he kept staring at Dara, studying her, watching her as if expecting something from her.

"We have to continue the Truth or Dare game," Dara suggested as we returned to the living room.

"Not me," I said, yawning. "I'm ready for bed." I couldn't wait to get out of my wet clothes and under some warm blankets.

Everyone seemed really tired. Dara shrugged and gave in. "See you guys in the morning," she said.

We all headed to our rooms. The boys made their way to their rooms at the end of the long hall to the left. Carly, Jenny, and I went to our rooms in the other wing.

I pulled off my sweater and jeans and tossed them onto a chair. Shivering, I pulled on a long flannel nightshirt.

A few minutes later I was coming out of the bathroom when I heard noises from the living room. Footsteps. Someone moving around in there.

I padded down the hall and peered into the room. The fireplace was dark except for a few purple embers. But in the dim light from the glass door, I could see Dara pulling on a blue coat.

"Dara, where are you going?" I called in a loud whisper.

She turned, startled by my voice. "Just out to the

woodshed," she replied, unrolling a pair of wet gloves and struggling to pull them on. "To get firewood for tomorrow morning."

"Want some help?" I offered.

She shook her head. "No, thanks, April. You've already changed. It won't take me long. Go get into bed, okay? See you in the morning."

"See you in the morning," I replied sleepily. I heard the door open and close as I started back to my room.

"What's going on?" a voice called.

I turned to see Tony halfway down the boy's hall. "Dara went out for firewood," I told him.

He nodded and returned to his room.

I wonder why Dara dislikes Tony so much, I thought, stepping back into my room and closing the door behind me. I wonder if they used to go out.

I didn't have long to think about it. I was asleep a few seconds after lowering my head on the pillow.

On Saturday morning I sat up in bed and gazed at the window. The gray glare from outside made the glass gleam like silver.

Had it snowed enough for us to go skiing?

I climbed out of bed, stretched, and eagerly crossed the room to the window. "Wow!" I cried out loud. "It's a blizzard!"

I stared out at the snow. It blanketed the ground and the trees. It must be a foot deep already, I realized. A deep drift appeared to climb up toward my window ledge.

And the snow continued to fall, a shimmering

curtain of tiny white flakes, swirled in all directions by a gusting wind.

"A blizzard!" I repeated happily. "Look out, slopes! Here I come!"

I dressed quickly. Brushed my teeth and my hair. And hurried to breakfast.

Unfortunately, my good mood lasted only until I reached the kitchen.

And received the frightening news that two of us were missing.

chapter

8

*E*verything seemed normal at first.

Tony leaned over the counter, pouring coffee into the coffeemaker. Carly stood at the glass door, casually pulling her auburn hair back as she gazed out at the falling snow.

Jenny and Ken were huddled by the radio.

"Good morning!" I called cheerily.

But they both raised a finger to their lips, signaling for me to be quiet. I stepped closer to hear what they were listening so intently to on the radio.

"The snow is expected to drop another eight-to-ten inches," the radio voice was saying. "That's the good news. But the bad news for skiers is that the lifts will not be running due to the high winds."

I groaned in disappointment.

Ken frowned and shook his head. "I thought the ski lifts *always* ran," he complained. "What are we supposed to do all day?"

"Climb up the slope on our hands and knees, I guess," I joked.

Jenny angrily clicked off the radio. "I don't believe it," she muttered unhappily. "If it's too windy to ski, what *are* we going to do?"

Carly was the first to notice that Dara was missing. "Where is she? She was telling me last night about what an earlybird she is," Carly declared.

"Josh isn't up yet, either," I commented.

Tony poured water into the coffeemaker and turned it on. "I'm starving," he announced, starting to pull open kitchen cabinets. "What's for breakfast? Could anyone go for eggs and bacon?"

"Oink, oink," Carly muttered.

"Hey—I *like* bacon!" Tony protested.

"I could make some pancakes," Jenny offered. "If we have the ingredients."

"Do you think we should check on Dara?" I asked, pulling open the refrigerator door. I took out a carton of orange juice and began searching the cabinets over the sink for the juice glasses.

"She needs her beauty sleep, I guess," Tony replied, snickering.

"Are there any eggs?" Jenny asked me. "Check the fridge. Can anyone find any pancake mix or anything?"

We all pitched in to make breakfast. I don't think

any of us were really worried about Dara: Everyone seemed in a good mood as we stuffed ourselves on pancakes and syrup, bacon, juice, and coffee.

"I think the wind is dying down," Ken reported, studying the falling snow through the glass door.

"Yaaaay!" Jenny cheered. "We've *got* to ski today. I don't think I can wait another day!"

"Dara is missing a great breakfast," I muttered, wiping maple syrup off my chin with my napkin. "Josh, too."

As I said, we weren't too worried.

But as we were rinsing the dishes and loading them into the dishwasher, it did seem strange that Dara hadn't appeared. "She likes to be the good hostess," I said. "It's not like her to skip breakfast."

"What do you want to do? Think we should go wake her up?" Ken asked, turning off the sink faucets. He dried his hands on a dish towel, then pushed his brown hair off his forehead with one hand.

"Don't go in there. Let her sleep," Tony replied. He had joined Carly in front of the glass door. "She's real cranky if you wake her."

"How do *you* know?" Carly demanded suspiciously.

Tony laughed. "I'm just guessing. Dara is *always* cranky, right?"

"Only to you, Tony," Jenny said under her breath.

"I think we should wake Dara up," I insisted. "She'll probably be embarrassed that she didn't get up in time to have breakfast with us."

"You can do it," Ken said to me. "We don't all have

to go—do we?" He clicked on the radio. "Maybe there's better news about the weather."

"I'll go with you, April," Jenny volunteered.

"Okay. Let's do it," I said. I closed the dishwasher. Then, drying my hands on the sides of my sweatshirt, I led the way down the hall to Dara's room.

The door was closed. Jenny knocked.

No reply.

"Hey—Dara!" I called in. "Rise and shine! Dara—it's morning!"

Still no reply.

"Dara—can you hear us?" Jenny shouted. She knocked again. "Dara?"

When we still didn't receive a reply, I turned the doorknob and pushed open the door.

Jenny and I both gasped.

"She's not here!" Jenny exclaimed.

We stepped into the room and glanced around. "Weird," I murmured. "Her bed—" I pointed. Her bed was made.

Did Dara get up early and make it? Or did that mean she hadn't slept in it last night?

"The room is so neat," Jenny commented, moving toward the bed. "Did she hang up—?"

"Her overnight bag!" I cried, pointing. It stood beside the dresser. It hadn't been unpacked. It hadn't been touched.

"Jenny, I—I don't think Dara slept here last night," I stammered.

"But that's impossible!" Jenny exclaimed. Her blue eyes narrowed in confusion.

"It's definitely weird," I said. I led the way back out to the hall. "Hey, Dara!" I called. "Dara—are you here?"

No answer.

"Let's check out Josh's room," I suggested. I didn't wait for Jenny to reply. I jogged down the hall.

"Did you find her?" Ken called as Jenny and I passed the kitchen.

"Not yet," I called back.

Jenny and I trotted down the other long hallway to the room Ken and Josh shared. The door was open halfway, so we peeked in.

"Josh?" I called softly.

The dark wood bunk bed stood against the wall. I remembered that Josh wanted to sleep in the top bunk.

No sign of him. No one in there.

"Weird," I repeated, shaking my head. Jenny shrugged. She appeared as puzzled as I was.

We returned to the kitchen. "Did you guys see Josh this morning when you woke up?" I asked.

Tony turned away from the window. "I didn't look for him," he replied, rubbing his chin.

Ken was switching from radio station to radio station, searching for some good music. "I didn't see him, either," he said.

"But he slept in there with you last night—right?" I asked Ken.

Ken scratched his head. "Yeah. I guess."

"But weren't you in the bottom bunk?" I asked him.

"I fell asleep real fast," Ken replied. "I guess Josh

was up there. I don't really know. I'm such a heavy sleeper."

"Well, I just think it's very weird that two of us aren't here this morning," I said. "And both of their beds look as if they weren't slept in."

"They'll show up," Tony replied casually. He slid his arm around Carly's shoulders and turned back to the window. "They probably went for a walk."

"In this blizzard?" I cried.

But Tony's words reminded me of something. After we had all gone to bed, Dara had gone out for firewood. Had she brought the firewood in?

I made my way into the living room and examined the fireplace area. No. The basket lay empty, except for a few twigs. The fireplace stood empty, too.

No firewood.

"Hey, guys," I called, my voice shaking as I hurried back to the kitchen. "We've got a little problem."

"Have you heard this song?" Ken asked, cranking up the radio. "Isn't it awesome?"

"Ken—!" I cried impatiently. "I think something strange has happened. Please—" I clicked off the radio.

Tony and Carly came over to the table. "What's up?" Tony asked.

"I saw Dara going out late last night," I told them. "She said she was going to the woodshed for firewood. But there isn't any wood by the fireplace."

Jenny let out a low cry. I saw her eyes narrow in fear. "Do you think—?"

"I think we should look outside," I said, fighting down my own fear. "Just in case—"

I didn't finish my sentence. I didn't really know what I was thinking. I only knew that I had a growing feeling of dread inside me.

Something was very wrong. Josh was gone. Dara was gone. Their beds appeared unslept in.

We hurried to the front and quickly grabbed up coats, the first coat we could. Then we stepped out the door, into the blowing snow.

I had taken only a few steps when I realized that something else was wrong.

I blinked once. Twice. Thinking maybe the heavy sheets of snow falling in front of me had confused me.

But no. I was right.

"Look—" I cried, pointing to the snow-covered driveway.

The *empty* driveway.

"The Jeep—it's gone."

chapter
9

"Dara and Josh probably left together," Tony said.

I stared across the kitchen at him, trying to decide if he was serious. No way to tell. I rubbed my nose, still frozen and numb.

We had hurried back into the house, eager to get out of the frigid, swirling winds. The snow was coming down so hard and fast, it had covered up the Jeep tire tracks—and any footprints.

Now we huddled together around the table in the warm kitchen, staring out at the darkening sky. And thinking hard, trying to figure out why two of us were missing, along with the only vehicle.

"Why do you say that?" I asked Tony. "What makes you think they drove off together?"

A strange smile spread on Tony's face. "They used to go together," he said softly. "Did you know that?"

"No. But it wasn't anything serious—was it?" I asked.

"Dara wasn't interested," Tony continued. "But I think Josh still is. Did you see the hurt looks he kept giving Dara all last night?"

"So you think—" I started.

"I think they took a drive. You know. To talk things over," Tony said, glancing at Carly.

Carly never stopped fiddling with her masses of auburn hair. Now she was twisting a strand of it, curling it tensely around her fingers. "You think they went for a drive in *this* weather?" she asked Tony.

"It's possible," he muttered.

We all gazed out the glass door. The sky was nearly as dark as night out there. The snow appeared pale blue as it swirled and spun to the ground. The wind howled around the sharp corners of the house.

"I'm putting on the kettle," Jenny said, rubbing the sleeves of her ski sweater. "I can't seem to get warm."

"They probably drove to one of the ski lodges," Tony continued. "There are a whole bunch of them just down the highway."

"But Dara wouldn't take the Jeep and go without leaving us a note," I insisted. "She just wouldn't."

"She would if it was an impulsive, spur-of-the-moment thing," Jenny replied, filling the big blue kettle with water from the tap.

"Yeah. Maybe Dara figured she and Josh would be back by now. But they had to stay at the ski lodge because of the snowy roads," Ken suggested.

"Then she would call us," I replied. I shoved my chair back from the table and stood up. I suddenly realized my heart was pounding. My hands were cold as ice.

"Listen, guys," I said, trying not to sound frightened. "I really think we have to call the police."

"No!" Tony cried loudly. Too loudly. He glanced across the table at Carly. "I mean—no," he said, more quietly this time. "We can't call the police."

"Huh? Why not?" I demanded.

"Well . . ." Tony glanced again at Carly. "You see . . . it would be kind of embarrassing," he said slowly, keeping his eyes on hers. "I mean, it would get Carly and me in major trouble."

He swallowed hard and turned to me. "Our parents don't know we came up here," he confessed.

"If we call the police, our parents will find out," Carly added. "Can't we just wait an hour or two? I'm sure Dara will call."

I sighed and sat back down. I couldn't decide what we should do. I had a very bad feeling.

"Don't worry about Dara," Tony assured me. "She's been coming up here since she was a kid. She knows every road and back road. I'm telling you, she and Josh are at a ski lodge right now. Safe and warm."

I studied Tony's face. To my surprise, he had beads of sweat running down his forehead.

Why is he sweating like that? I asked myself. Why is he so determined to keep me from calling the police?

Does he have *another* reason?

I felt a shiver of fear. I'm frightened of Tony, I realized.

He saw me staring at him. I turned away. Turned to the glass door—in time to see something tumble off the roof.

It hit the snow with a soft *thud*—and I started to scream.

chapter
10

My horrified scream echoed through the kitchen.

"April—what's wrong?" Jenny cried shrilly from the stove. She dropped the teakettle onto the burner and hurried to the table.

Ken dived around the table and grabbed my shoulders. "Are you okay?" he demanded. "What's wrong?"

I pointed to the sliding door with a trembling finger. "Did you see it?" I stammered. "Something fell. I saw it fall. From the roof!"

Tony got to the door first. He pressed his face against the glass and peered out into the darkness.

He stood there for a long time without moving.

"See it?" I asked in a hushed whisper. "Tony—can you see it?"

"I don't see anything, April," he called back to me.

Carly pressed beside him. Her blue eyes narrowed in concern. Jenny hurried to the door, too.

"It was a big clump of snow," Jenny reported. She stepped away from the glass door and turned back to me. "Are you okay? That's all you saw. Just snow."

"Yeah. It blew down off the roof," Tony said. He rolled his eyes. "You're losing it," he murmured.

I slumped over the table. "I—I'm really sorry," I said. "I'm so worried about Dara and Josh. I guess I—"

I could feel my face turning red. I felt like a total jerk. I could see all of them—even Jenny—staring at me as if I were some kind of mental case.

April is really messed up. April is starting to see things.

That's what they were all thinking.

"Hey—no big deal. We're all worried about Dara and Josh," Tony said, turning to stare out at the falling snow. "But they're okay. I *know* they are. I know Dara," he added dryly. "Dara is *always* okay."

We made ham and turkey sandwiches for lunch. But none of us really felt much like eating.

The wind continued to howl, and the snow hurtled down, sheet after sheet of it. The lights in the house flickered. Then dimmed. But they didn't go out.

Jenny and I searched for candles—just in case. We

found a box of them in a linen closet and put them on the coffee table in the living room.

I felt so stressed out and scared. Every sound made me jump. I wanted to cover my ears from the howling wind.

Jenny, Ken, and I found a deck of cards and settled down on the living room couch to play gin rummy—just to take our minds off the fact that we were waiting, waiting, waiting to hear from Dara and Josh.

Gin rummy is such a boring game. And I think there were some cards missing from our deck.

"We're not playing with a full deck!" Ken declared. His idea of a joke.

Jenny and I groaned.

Tony and Carly were in the kitchen. They said they wanted to make popcorn. But I think they were making out. They couldn't keep their hands off each other for more than a few minutes.

Jenny yawned.

"Want to do something else?" I asked.

"Anything but Truth or Dare," Ken snapped. He flashed me a meaningful glance.

So he *did* figure out what I meant last night! I realized.

Ken knows that I know about the girl on Sumner Island.

"Get some music on the radio," Jenny suggested.

"Yeah. Good idea. It's too quiet in here," Ken said. He climbed to his feet and started to cross the room—when we heard the knocking.

Loud knocking.

I jumped to my feet. "It's coming from the back!" I cried. "It must be Dara and Josh!"

The three of us bolted to the kitchen. Tony and Carly had already reached the door. As I entered the kitchen behind Ken and Jenny, they were peering out into the back.

"Who's there?" I called eagerly. "Is it Dara and Josh?"

Tony turned away from the door, a puzzled expression on his face. "It's no one," he replied. "No one there."

"But we heard knocking," Jenny said, joining Tony and Carly at the door.

"So did we," Carly told her. "But take a look for yourself. There's no one out there."

How weird, I thought. What made that sound? I knew we hadn't imagined it.

Ken turned to Tony. "Did *you* do it?" he accused. "Another joke to scare us?"

"Excuse me?" Tony's mouth dropped open. "No way, man!" he declared. "I'm as worried about Dara as you are. I'm not pulling any dumb jokes."

Ken studied Tony's face for a moment, then turned back to me. The three of us made our way back to the living room.

"We need a fire in here," I murmured, lowering myself into a leather armchair and gazing at the dark fireplace.

"Maybe we should all go out and collect firewood," Ken replied. "At least it would give us something to do. The woodshed is probably—"

He stopped when the knocking started again.

Loud pounding on the door. From the back of the house.

Once again we raced to the kitchen.

Carly and Tony stood by the door, puzzled frowns on their faces. "No one there," Tony reported. "No one!"

chapter

11

"Someone had to be knocking," Ken said, scratching the back of his head. "We heard it plain as day." Once again he stared accusingly at Tony.

Tony swept a hand back through his wavy hair. He sighed. "Carly and I heard it, too. But take a look. There's no one out there."

"Maybe the wind is blowing something against the house," Jenny suggested. "Or maybe it's a window shutter banging in the wind."

"The house doesn't have window shutters," Tony told her.

I stepped up to the door and pressed my forehead

against the cool glass. The snow was tumbling down, billowing sheets of snow so thick, I could barely see the backyard. I could barely see past the small back porch.

"No footprints," I reported. I turned to the driveway. It ended in a low carport on the side of the house. "And no sign of Dara's Jeep."

My voice caught in my throat as I said those words. "No sign of . . . anything."

A chill ran down my back. I turned away from the window.

And the knocking started again.

One loud knock. Then a second.

"I think it's coming from the back porch," I said, shielding my eyes with both hands, squinting against the snow to see better.

It was like trying to see through cotton.

The knocking repeated. A loud, steady banging from very close by.

"Oh. I see it!" I cried. "It's the ski locker. On the porch."

"Huh?" Jenny pushed up beside me and stared out into the darkness.

I pointed to the tall green metal locker on the side of the porch. "See? The door has come loose. It's banging against the locker."

"Well, at least one mystery is solved," Jenny said, stepping back from the door. She let out a relieved sigh.

"Let's go close it," Ken urged. "If we don't, the banging will drive us crazy."

"Just leave it," Jenny told him. "We can close it after the snow stops falling."

"No. Come on." Ken tugged her arm. "I can't stand the noise."

"We don't *all* have to go out there," Tony protested. "It won't take five of us to close a locker door."

"I'll go with you," I told Ken. "I could use some cold, fresh air."

Ken and I grabbed the first coats we saw, pulled them over our shoulders, and made our way out through the back door. As we stepped onto the back porch, the wind blew the falling snow into our faces, forcing us to shield our eyes.

"Wow. I feel as if I'm in one of those snow globes!" Ken exclaimed. "You know. The glass balls you shake and the snow floats in every direction."

"Yeah. It's so windy, you can't tell if the snow is falling up or down!" I agreed.

Our boots sank into the deep, wet snow as we stepped over to the ski locker.

The metal door banged hard against the locker. Then the wind blew the door open again.

I brushed snow off my eyebrows and followed Ken to the locker. He reached for the door, but the wind blew it open farther.

Ken and I both cried out, startled, as something toppled out of the ski locker and landed in the snow with a *thud*.

"Noooo!" A horrified wail escaped my throat as I stared down.

Stared down at a blue face under a tangle of streaked blond hair.

Stared down at a stiff, lifeless body.

Stared down at Dara's frozen corpse.

chapter

12

I grabbed Ken's arm. Held on tightly.

My legs gave way. I felt myself start to sink. To sink into the snow. To sink into the white. To fall and fall and fall.

Dara's blue eyes stared up at me accusingly. Her mouth was frozen open in a wide O of horror. Of pain. The snow whirled around us. Holding us in place. Freezing Ken and me. Freezing us like Dara. Stiff. Terrified.

I felt my throat tighten. *I'm trapped*, I thought. Trapped inside a whirring white cyclone. Trapped with Dara. Trapped with Dara's dead body. Her dead face. Her dead eyes.

Blue. So blue and cold.

Her hair tossed and shivered in the wind.

The only thing that moved.

And then Ken suddenly pulled away from me. I thought I would fall. Fall forward onto Dara's blue corpse.

But somehow I caught my balance.

Ken bent over with a groan to examine Dara's body. Grabbing on to the collar of the parka, Ken slowly lifted up Dara's body slightly. Dara's head dropped backward.

Squinting through the white, gauzy curtain of snow, I saw the dark stain on the shoulder of her parka.

The dark puddle of dried blood.

"Ohhhhh!" Another cry escaped my throat as I saw the hatchet. Buried between her shoulder blades.

Buried so deep that just a glint of the metal showed above the parka.

Murdered. Dara was murdered with a hatchet.

Dara. Murdered in the snow. So cold. So cold she's blue.

My stomach lurched. I started to gag.

I stumbled off the porch. Snow up over my boots. I bent over and started to vomit. Retching up the horror. My entire body heaved and trembled.

I shut my eyes tight. I gasped in the cold, wet air.

And felt Ken's hands, gentle on my shoulders. Leading me back onto the porch. I heard the glass door sliding. Felt him guide me back into the kitchen.

Felt the warmth. The aroma of popcorn.

My body still trembling.

I'll never be normal. The words forced their way through my mind. *Never be normal again.*

"What happened?" Jenny asked. "What's wrong with April?"

"Dara's dead," Ken replied in a whisper.

I heard shocked gasps. I heard Carly scream.

I still couldn't see them. I could see only blue. Dara's blue face. Her blue face, frozen in such horror, such pain.

"She's been murdered," Ken told them.

More gasps and shrieks. I opened my eyes to see Jenny sobbing, tears already running down her cheeks. Tony comforting Carly.

I leaned back against the wall. My knees still shaking, my legs so weak and rubbery. "We—we've got to call the police," I choked out. "Now."

Tony gave Carly a meaningful glance. I knew he was worried about his parents finding out that he had sneaked up here with Carly for the weekend.

But that didn't matter anymore.

Dara had a hatchet in her back. Dara had been murdered.

"We have no choice now!" I said to Tony. I didn't mean to scream, to sound so shrill. But I couldn't help it. I swallowed hard and held my breath to force down my nausea.

Slumped at the table, Jenny buried her face in her hands. Her shoulders heaved up and down as she sobbed.

Ken let out a sigh. "April is right," he murmured.

"We have no choice. We have to call the police—right away."

We all cried out as a gust of wind blew through the kitchen. Ken and I had been so upset, we hadn't closed the sliding door.

I turned to the door. Lying stiffly in the snow, Dara stared in at us. Her unblinking blue eyes seemed to glare at me. Accuse me. Her hair fluttered in the wind. A covering of snow had fallen over it, over the shoulders of the parka. Over the blood-soaked shoulder.

"Close the door!" I shrieked, covering my eyes with both hands. "Close it!"

Ken pulled the door shut and turned the lock.

Dara continued to stare in at us from the other side of the glass.

I turned away—to find that Tony had moved to the wall phone. He held the receiver in one hand.

"Call them," I instructed him. "Tony—call the police."

He shook his head, a strange blank expression on his face. "I'm sorry," he said softly. "I can't."

chapter

13

"*T*ony—what are you *saying?*" I demanded.

"We can't call the police," he repeated, replacing the receiver. "The line is dead."

"Huh?" I cried. "You mean—?"

"No dial tone at all," Tony said, shaking his head. "The storm must have blown down the wires."

"But—but—" I sputtered.

"We'll have to *walk* to town," Ken suggested, gazing out at the sky. The dark clouds appeared even lower.

It could snow like this for days, I thought.

My entire body convulsed in a cold shudder. I wrapped my arms around my chest and, feeling weak and frightened, leaned back against the wall.

"Or ski—we *could* ski to town!" Ken exclaimed.

"We'd never make it," Carly said, tugging tensely at a strand of auburn hair. "Not without a car. Even if we made it down the hill, how far could we get in this blinding snowstorm? We'd freeze before we'd reach the ski slopes, let alone town."

"How far is town?" I asked Tony.

"Couple of miles," he muttered. "Maybe a mile past the slopes. There are some ski lodges before town. But I don't think we could get to them, either. At least, not until the snow stops coming down so hard."

"Maybe we could hitch a ride with someone," I suggested.

The idea was greeted by silence.

"What kind of a nut would be out driving today?" Tony finally replied. He walked over to the refrigerator and pulled out a can of Coke. "At least we've got enough food and supplies."

"But there's a *murderer* out there!" I cried shrilly. "We can't just sit here and do nothing! Someone killed Dara. And—and—oh!"

I clapped a hand over my mouth.

Josh.

In my horror over Dara, I had totally forgotten him.

"What about Josh?" I choked out. "We're going to find his body, too—aren't we!"

"No!" Carly shrieked. "Please—!"

"We are," I insisted, shaking all over. "Whoever killed Dara probably killed Josh, too. And whoever it is, is out there." I pointed to the door.

"But there are no footprints!" Carly protested. "If someone was in the backyard and killed Dara and Josh, wouldn't there be footprints?"

"Maybe the snow covered them up," Jenny said, wiping her tear-swollen cheeks. "It's snowing so fast. Footprints would disappear in minutes!"

"She's right," Carly agreed.

"No. She's wrong," Tony said. He walked to the glass door and stared out.

I couldn't bear to see Dara staring in at us. So I lowered my gaze to the floor.

"You and Carly are both wrong," Tony said to me. "There's no killer waiting out there. Because the killer was Josh."

"Excuse me?" I cried. I felt dizzy. The floor seemed to be tilting first one way, then the other. I slid my back along the wall and lowered myself to a sitting position on the kitchen floor.

"It's obvious," Tony said, moving away from the door and sitting down at the table beside Carly. He took a long drink from the Coke can. "Josh killed Dara. Then he drove away in Dara's Jeep."

"But why?" I blurted out. "Why would Josh kill Dara?"

Tony shrugged. "Who knows?"

Ken stepped over to the phone and lifted the receiver to his ear. He sighed and set it back down. "Still out."

"What are we going to do?" Jenny wailed. "We're trapped here. There are no other houses around. The snow is too deep to walk. It's snowing too hard to ski for help. We're trapped!"

"We'll get some firewood. We'll keep a big fire going," Tony replied. "We'll stay warm and comfortable. The snow will stop. The phone will be fixed. We'll be okay, Jenny. If we stay calm and don't panic, we'll all be okay."

"Let's search Josh's room," I suggested. I pulled myself to my feet. "Let's see if we can find any clues there. Anything at all."

"If Josh took his bag, then we *know* he killed Dara and drove away," Ken said.

"I can't believe Josh wasn't up in that bunk last night," Ken said, shaking his head. "If only I wasn't such a heavy sleeper . . ." His voice trailed off.

All five of us trooped down the hall to the room he had shared with Josh. I clicked on the ceiling light and stepped into the middle of the large room.

Outside, the sky had darkened to evening charcoal. The wind howled around the corners of the house.

The room was chilly, colder than the other rooms. Chilly and damp smelling.

"Look—Josh's bag!" I cried, pointing.

The blue canvas bag stood beside the bunk bed. Ken and I dropped down onto our knees and unzipped it.

Ken pulled it open, and I gazed inside.

"It's full," I announced, turning back to Jenny, Tony, and Carly. "His clothes—they're all here."

"Huh? What does that *mean?*" Carly cried.

"It means he drove off without his stuff," Tony

replied, walking over to peer in the bag. "Maybe he was so crazed, so messed up after killing Dara, he didn't even think of taking his bag."

"Maybe . . ." I replied doubtfully. "Or maybe it means that . . ." The words caught in my throat. A heavy feeling of dread crept up from my stomach.

"Maybe it means that Josh was murdered, too." Ken finished my thought for me. He turned the bag over and dumped everything onto the floor.

We sifted through it quickly.

Just clothes. An extra sweater. A ski outfit. Gray sweatpants. A small bag containing a toothbrush, deodorant, tissues, and a comb.

Nothing the least bit interesting.

I jumped to my feet. I climbed onto the lower bed and examined the top bunk. The blanket was smooth and tucked in tightly at the sides. "Nothing up here," I reported. "I really don't think he was ever in this bed."

I lowered myself to the floor. "I guess we should check out Dara's room, too," I told them.

Every time I said Dara's name, I pictured her stiff, frozen body. Her blue face, twisted in pain and horror. The hatchet, buried so deep in her shoulder blades.

We made our way silently to Dara's room. In the hallway next to Dara's door, I stopped in front of a low wicker table.

The table contained a slender blue vase filled with pink and purple dried wildflowers. Beside it stood a framed photograph. It showed Dara, a few years younger, in a bright yellow ski outfit. Her mother and father, also in bright ski outfits, stood behind her, smiling into the camera.

The three of them looked so happy.

Gazing at the photo, I almost burst into tears.

Biting my lower lip, I forced myself to turn away from the happy family in the photograph and stepped into Dara's bedroom.

Ken clicked on a tall lamp beside the bed, and we began to look around. Posters of Olympic skiers lined one wall. Shelves along the opposite wall were crammed with books and old magazines, board games, tapes and CDs.

The bed was covered in a black-and-white checkered quilt. Beside the bed stood an oak nightstand. A paperback book lay open, pages down. Beside the book, I spotted a folded-up sheet of white paper.

Ken pulled open the door to the closet and peered in. The others were examining the cluttered shelves.

I picked up the sheet of paper, unfolded it, and read it quickly.

"Oh, I don't believe it!" I cried. The paper trembled in my hand. Everyone turned back to me.

"I know who killed Dara," I said.

chapter
_____
14

*T*hey clustered around, and I read the letter out loud. It was written in red ballpoint. The handwriting was sloppy, hard to read. Hurried. There were red smudges where the ink had leaked.

I held the page under the lamp and began to read in a soft, trembling voice:

Dear Dara,

I can't go on like this anymore.

No matter how cruel you are to me, I always take it. You humiliated me tonight. How could you?

I always thought you were someone worth

caring about. But I guess I made a big mistake.

But I have to talk to you one more time. I
won't take no for an answer.

Meet me at midnight. Alone!!!

Josh

Jenny grabbed the letter from my hand and read it
again quickly. Ken and Carly read it over Jenny's
shoulder.

When Jenny handed the letter back to me, her face
had gone pale. Her normally dark lips were white. Her
chin trembled. "We—we have to get *out* of here!" she
cried.

"Jenny—why?" I asked, folding the letter carefully.

"Well, don't you see?" Jenny asked impatiently.
"He'll remember he wrote this letter. Josh will remember it. He'll turn around. He'll come back here.
And he'll kill us all because we read it! Because we
know!"

She began sobbing loudly again.

"Jenny—" I said softly. I reached out to comfort
her. But she took off, running past me into the hall.

"Jenny—!" I kept calling her name as I jogged after
her. Into the kitchen.

She picked up the phone receiver. She started
frantically punching numbers. "Come on! Come on!
Come on!" she cried, punching the numbers harder
and harder. "You've got to work! You've *got* to!"

She slammed the dead receiver against the wall.

I moved quickly to her and wrapped her in a hug. Her entire body was trembling. "Jenny," I whispered. "We'll be okay. Really. We'll be okay."

"Josh will come back!" she sobbed. "He'll come back and murder us all, just like Dara."

I glanced over my shoulder to see Ken, Tony, and Carly entering the kitchen.

"We've got to stay calm," Ken warned, coming over to Jenny and me, his eyes locked on Jenny. "We can't panic, Jenny. It won't help us. We have to stay calm so we can think clearly."

"He's going to come back!" Jenny cried. I could see she had totally lost it. I felt so helpless. What could I do to calm her down?

I was just as frightened as Jenny. And I was just as worried that Josh might remember the letter and come back for it.

But we couldn't leave the house. The snow was too deep and coming down too hard. The winds were freezing and nearly strong enough to blow us over.

We had no car. No phone. No neighbors.

We were trapped.

Jenny had every right to be frightened.

"Hey—there might be a gun in the house!" Tony declared. His words snapped me back from my frightening thoughts.

"Excuse me?" I asked, turning to him.

He finished his Coke and crushed the can in his hand. "Did anyone see a gun anywhere in the house? Dara's Dad used to keep a pistol here. I wonder if he still does. We should protect ourselves. You know. In case Josh comes back."

I just stared blankly at Tony. I couldn't believe he wanted to find a gun. Did he know anything about guns? I wasn't sure I wanted Tony to have a gun.

I realized I still didn't trust him. He hadn't really done anything wrong. Call it a hunch. I just didn't trust him.

"I haven't seen a gun anywhere," Ken told him.

"Maybe we should look for it," Tony replied.

"Tony, please!" Carly pleaded. She had dropped down next to Jenny at the table and had been holding Jenny's hand, trying to calm her.

"What's your problem?" Tony snapped at her. "Don't you think I know how to use a gun?"

"Aren't things scary enough, Tony?" Carly cried. "Why make it even more frightening?"

Tony scowled and walked into the living room. I could hear him moving around in there, pulling out drawers, opening cabinets. I hoped he didn't find a gun.

Jenny turned to me, tears rolling down her cheeks, her chin still quivering. "Do you think Josh will come back to get his letter?" she asked.

"I—I really don't know," I told her.

Outside the glass door Dara—covered by snow—seemed to stare in at us. And the snow continued to fall.

I knew I wouldn't be able to get to sleep that night. And I was right.

Lying in bed with the blankets pulled up to my throat, I tried reading. But I had brought only a scary thriller to read. And I wasn't exactly in the mood for a thriller!

Every sound in the house, every shift of the wind made my heart skip a beat.

It had been such a long, dreadful day. The hours had stretched on until they seemed like weeks. We were all tense, frightened, upset.

We had pulled Dara's frozen body into the garage, out of sight. But I still saw her blue, snow-covered face, her blank, staring eyes every time I thought about her.

I settled my head into the pillow and shut my eyes. I concentrated on relaxing my body. Every muscle seemed hard and tight.

I concentrated on relaxing my foot muscles. Then my leg muscles. I breathed slowly, steadily. "Calm, April. Calm. Calm," I kept telling myself, trying to soothe myself to sleep.

I had nearly drifted off when I heard the creak of the floorboards, the sound of footsteps in the living room.

My entire body went rigid. I had to force myself to breathe

I listened hard.

Yes. Someone had entered the living room. Some-one was moving slowly, quietly.

Someone didn't want to be heard.

The creaking floorboards gave him away

I forced myself to take another breath. I gripped the blankets with both hands, squeezed until my hands hurt.

Josh is back, I realized.

Josh has come back.

Come back to kill the rest of us?

chapter

15

*S*hivering, I lowered my feet to the floor. I crept out of bed and pulled on my robe.

I struggled to breathe normally. It felt as if my heart had leaped into my throat.

I made my way out into the dark hall and listened. Silence. Then a single creaking footstep.

I saw a glimmer of light from the living room.

Did Josh have a flashlight?

As my eyes adjusted to the dark hallway, I searched for a weapon. Anything. Anything I could use to protect myself.

I spotted a ski pole propped against the wall near the corner. I picked it up, gripping the handle tightly in my cold, clammy hand.

Will it protect me against Josh? I wondered.

Yes. If I take him by surprise.

I crept quickly down the dark hallway, keeping my back pressed against the wall. I suddenly felt cold all over, as if my fear had frozen my skin.

I stopped just outside the living room doorway. Struggling to catch my breath, I leaned into the doorway and peered into the room.

Where is he? I wondered. I heard him moving around in here.

I stared into the darkness, my eyes darting around the room.

I took a cautious step away from the wall.

He moved so quickly, I couldn't cry out. Couldn't resist.

I felt him beside me. Hidden in the deep shadows.

And then he leaped forward, grabbed me, and pulled me roughly into the darkness with him.

chapter

16

The ski pole fell from my hand and clattered to the floor.

I struggled to pull away. But he grasped me tightly and jerked me into the center of the room. "Let go—!" My plea came out in a choked whisper.

He reached one hand out and clicked on a lamp.

"Tony!" I cried. "What are you *doing?*"

As he let go of me, his face twisted in shock. His eyes went wide and his mouth dropped open. "Whoa!" he cried, taking a step back.

"Tony—!" I swallowed hard. My heart was pounding so fast, I could barely breathe.

"I—I thought—" he started. He slapped himself on the forehead. "I'm totally losing it!" he exclaimed.

"You scared me to death!" I finally managed to scream.

Tightening the belt on his robe, he shook his head. "I'm sorry, April. Really. I'm sorry. I thought—"

"What? What did you think?" I demanded. My fear began to fade, replaced by anger.

"I thought you were Josh," Tony said. "Sorry. I feel like a real jerk."

"But, Tony, it's the middle of the night," I protested. "What were you doing in here?"

"I heard noises," he explained, avoiding my hard stare. He dropped onto the arm of a leather armchair. "I thought it was Josh sneaking back into the house. So I came in here to investigate."

"And?" I demanded, crossing my arms over the front of my bathrobe.

"I heard footsteps," Tony continued, still avoiding my eyes. "So I crept over there." He pointed to the wall beside the doorway. "And I waited. When I grabbed you, I thought you were Josh. I really did."

He finally raised his eyes to mine. I think he was checking to see if I believed him or not.

I didn't believe him. Something about his story didn't ring true.

Maybe he was just sneaking off to meet Carly, I decided.

"Did you and Dara used to go out?" The words tumbled from my mouth. I guess the question had been on my mind.

His expression changed. He narrowed his eyes at me suspiciously. "Yeah. For a while," he replied. He shifted his weight on the chair arm. "A very short while. No one ever went out with Dara for very long."

I was surprised by Tony's bitter tone. I think he was trying to sound casual. But he couldn't keep the anger from his voice.

"It was a long time ago," he added with a shrug. "Why do you care?"

"I—I don't," I stammered, feeling embarrassed. "I was just curious."

"She didn't really hurt me," Tony continued. "Not the way she hurt Josh. She really messed Josh up." He sighed. "You read the letter. Why am I telling you this?"

Why *is* he telling me this? I wondered. Was he just confiding in me? Trying to be friendly?

Why did I find myself so suspicious of Tony?

I started to cough. My throat felt so dry. "Think I need some water," I told him.

He followed me into the kitchen. I clicked on the ceiling light and blinked against the sudden brightness. The dirty dinner dishes were piled high in the sink. We were all so frightened and unhappy, we hadn't had the energy to load them in the dishwasher.

Someone had spilled some spaghetti sauce and hadn't bothered to sponge it up. The dried red sauce ran down the front of the white counter like a blood-stain.

The drinking glasses were all dirty. I rinsed one out, then let the tap water run, waiting for it to get cold.

As I took a long drink, letting the cold water soothe my parched throat, I could feel Tony's eyes on my back. I shivered and turned around to face him, wiping water off my chin with one hand.

"You're really scared, aren't you," he said softly.

I nodded. "Yeah. Aren't you?"

He shrugged. "A little, I guess." He fiddled with the salt shaker on the counter, rolling it between his hands. "But we'll be okay, April," he continued. "The phone will be back by tomorrow. We'll phone the police and tell them about Josh. They'll find him. I'm sure he didn't get very far in this blizzard."

"Probably not," I murmured. I finished the glass of water and set it down on the sink.

"The police will help us find a way to get home," Tony continued. "We'll be okay."

"This was supposed to be a fun weekend," I said sadly. "It's been so awful. So frightening."

"Yeah. I know," Tony replied. He set the salt shaker back on the counter. "It sure didn't work out the way I planned." He snickered. A bitter laugh.

"Poor Dara," I murmured.

He didn't reply to that. He seemed to be deep in his own thoughts. Then finally he said, "Guess we should get some sleep. In the morning—"

He stopped suddenly. He let out a low gasp.

I followed his gaze. He was staring at the glass door.

I turned to the door. It took me a few seconds to recognize what I was seeing.

Then my hands jerked up to the sides of my face, and I started to scream.

Josh's frozen body. Snow-covered. Wide-eyed.

Josh's frozen body was pressed against the glass.

chapter
17

 M y screams brought Carly and Jenny running into the kitchen.

"April—what's wrong?" Jenny cried. "What's happening?"

Ken stumbled sleepily into the room, wearing striped pajamas, his hair matted to his forehead. "Who screamed?" he demanded.

I pointed to the glass door.

Josh's snow-covered face stared in at us. His hands were raised above his head and pressed against the glass, as if he were trying to push the door open.

Who killed Josh?

The question flashed through my mind, sent a cold shudder down my back.

Who killed Josh? How did he get outside the back door?

I screamed again when Josh started to move.

He pounded both fists against the glass.

At first I thought the wind was blowing his body against the door. But I quickly realized that Josh wasn't dead. He was alive—and struggling to get inside.

Tony reached the door first. He turned the lock, then slid it open.

A blast of cold air swept through the room as Josh staggered in. Tony instantly closed the door behind him.

Josh shook his entire body, like a dog after a bath. Snow flew onto the kitchen floor.

"Josh—what happened? Where were you?" Ken cried.

Josh didn't reply. He struggled to pull off his wet coat, but couldn't get his trembling hands to work the zipper. His glasses had steamed up. A layer of snow had caked in his hair. Even his eyebrows were covered with snow.

"I—I—help me!" Josh croaked.

He finally managed to unzip the heavy down coat. With great effort he pulled it off and let it fall to the floor.

"Don't try anything!" Tony warned him sharply. "We know what you did."

Josh pulled off his frosted glasses and blinked at Tony. He wiped the glasses on the front of his sweater. But they only smeared.

"I . . . need . . . something . . . hot." It seemed to take great effort for him to talk. His entire body trembled. His nose and ears were bright scarlet. I wondered if they were frostbitten.

"Something . . . hot. Please!" he begged. His legs gave out and he started to fall. He grabbed the counter with both hands and held himself up.

"I—I've been . . . walking . . . so far . . ." Josh said. He put on the wet eyeglasses. His eyes were wild and unfocused behind them.

Carly moved to the sink and filled the kettle. "He's really messed up," she muttered. "I'm making coffee for everyone. Instant is all we have left."

Josh lowered himself into a kitchen chair and gazed around the room. He seemed dazed. Totally out of it. He pulled chunks of hardened snow from his dark hair with one hand.

"Why did you kill Dara?" Tony demanded, stepping up beside him.

"Huh?" Josh didn't seem able to focus. He kept blinking his eyes. His entire body shuddered again. "So . . . cold," he murmured. He didn't even seem to hear Tony.

He pressed his hands against his red cheeks. "Numb," he muttered.

"Answer the question, Josh," Tony insisted sharply. "Why did you do it?"

Josh gazed up at Tony, a bewildered expression on his face. "Do it?"

"We found Dara's body," Tony said. "Why did you kill her?"

"Dara?" Josh shook his head. His eyes appeared to swim around behind the foggy glasses. "I'm sorry," he said. "I'm sorry."

"Sorry you did it?" Tony demanded.

"Sorry . . . I don't understand," Josh replied. "I'm . . . frozen. Been walking through the snow . . . all day."

And then he uttered a sharp cry. And stared up at Tony. I think Tony's words finally got through to him. "Dara?" Josh demanded. "What about Dara?"

"You tell us!" Tony snarled.

"What *about* her?" Josh insisted shrilly. "Tell me. What did you say? I thought you said—"

"She's dead!" Jenny cried, moving across the table from Josh. "Dara is dead—and you killed her!"

"No!" Josh protested, rising to his feet. The chair toppled backward and clattered to the floor. "I don't understand! I really don't understand!" He grabbed his forehead and rubbed it, as if rubbing away a sharp headache.

Carly slid a mug of black coffee in front of Josh. "Here. Drink this," she told him. She watched Josh take the mug between his hands. Then she turned back to the counter to prepare coffee for the rest of us.

Josh warmed his hands on the mug. Then he raised it to his lips, holding it between both trembling hands. The steam rose up from the mug and fogged his glasses. He took a long sip. Then another.

It appeared to revive him a little. He picked up the fallen chair and sat back down in it. His eyes locked on me. "Dara is dead? You're serious?"

I nodded. I stared back intently at him, studying his face. He was doing a good job of acting innocent, I thought. But we knew the truth.

We had found his letter and read it.

We knew the truth about Josh. And we knew why he had come back to Dara's house. To get the letter, the letter that proved his guilt.

The shaking hands, the snow-covered hair, the trembling and stammering—all an act. I knew it. We all knew it.

"How can Dara be dead?" Josh asked innocently.

"Josh, it's no good," I told him. "We found your letter to Dara. We know everything."

He didn't react to that at all. Didn't move a muscle.

"Why did you do it? Why?" Jenny shrieked. Ken moved over to her and put his arm around her shoulders.

Josh stared up at me. "What letter?" he demanded, still pretending to be confused.

I rolled my eyes. "The letter you wrote to Dara. You accidentally left it behind. We found it next to Dara's bed."

Josh shook his head hard, as if trying to clear it.

Carly set down the kettle and hurried from the kitchen. I heard her padding down the hall. A few seconds later she reappeared with the letter in her hand.

"Here it is," she told Josh breathlessly.

Josh took it eagerly from Carly's hand.

Tony moved quickly to grab Josh's wrist. "Don't try to destroy it," he warned. "Better let me hold it."

"I just want to read it!" Josh insisted.

I watched his eyes run quickly down the page. His expression became more and more bewildered as he read the letter.

When he raised his eyes to us, his face, which had been so red, had gone pale. "It's—it's a total lie!" Josh cried. "This isn't my handwriting. I didn't write this letter!"

chapter

18

"**Y**ou're a liar!" Jenny accused. "You've been lying ever since we let you in."

"I'm *not!*" Josh insisted. "This letter—"

"How can you pretend you didn't know Dara was dead?" Jenny demanded. "We're not total morons, Josh!"

Tony pulled the letter from Josh's trembling hand. "We're holding on to this," he said quietly. "This is evidence."

"Josh, there's no way you can lie your way out of this," Ken said sharply, his arm still around Jenny's shoulders. "We're calling the town police as soon as the phone line is fixed. You killed Dara and you tried to get away in her Jeep."

"No way!" Josh protested. His hand shook so violently, he spilled coffee from his mug. "I know it looks bad. I mean, taking the Jeep. Driving away. But I'm telling the truth. I didn't kill Dara, and I didn't write that letter."

"I think we should tie him up or lock him in a room," Tony said to me. He moved behind Josh's chair, blocking any try at escape.

I sighed. I glanced at the clock over the stove. Nearly two in the morning. "Let him tell his story first," I told Tony.

I grabbed a mug of coffee, poured milk into it, then sat down across from Josh at the table. The others gathered around.

I studied Josh as he began to talk. I was trying to read his eyes, trying to tell if anything he said was true.

"I was so messed up last night," he started, leaning over the table, spinning his coffee mug slowly between his hands. "I was so upset. I knew I wouldn't be able to sleep. I stayed dressed. I paced back and forth in the living room, getting more and more angry."

"Angry about what? About the Truth or Dare game?" I asked.

Josh nodded. "I just can't stand being made fun of. When Dara started to tell everyone that I was the worst kisser she had ever known, I really lost it. I *did* want to kill her then. I really did."

"So you admit it. You killed her!" Jenny broke in.

"Let him go on," I scolded her.

"I didn't." Josh insisted. "But I was so hurt. And so

embarrassed. I have a short fuse. I admit it. I can't stand to be teased. Especially not by Dara. I don't want to get into it now. But Dara already hurt me. A lot."

That's all in the letter, I told myself. *Josh doesn't mean to. But he's proving that he wrote that letter.*

"I just sort of lost it," Josh continued, twirling the coffee mug, staring down at it as he talked. "I wasn't thinking clearly. I was too angry. I decided to take Dara's Jeep and strand her here. I—I wanted to teach her a lesson."

"You taught her a lesson, all right," Ken said sarcastically.

"So I stole the keys and took the Jeep," Josh continued, ignoring him. "I left early in the morning. It was crazy. It was so totally crazy. I didn't remember my bag or anything. All I could think of was paying Dara back for hurting me. I drove like a madman. Through the snow. But I didn't get far."

"What happened?" I asked.

Josh took a long sip of coffee. "It was impossible to drive," he said. "I kept sliding off the road. The road to town was completely blocked off. So I ended up on some back road. I didn't know where it went or anything."

He shook his head and let out a weary sigh. "I slid into a deep drift. I couldn't get out. I tried everything. I was stuck. And it was snowing so hard, I couldn't even see where I was."

He took another sip of coffee, emptying the mug. "I

kept the engine on because I needed the heater. But the gas tank was nearly empty. So I had to turn it off. I waited for a car or truck to come by. You know. To rescue me. But the road was empty. No one. Not a single car. I sat there for an hour or two. But I knew I couldn't sit there much longer. I'd freeze to death."

"So you started to walk?" I asked.

Josh nodded. "I left the Jeep and started to walk. I walked for a long time—then realized I was heading in the wrong direction. So I doubled back. I—I didn't realize how far I had gone."

He shook his head sadly. "I wanted to come back to the house and apologize to everyone. I had been such a jerk. I wanted to apologize for taking the Jeep. I walked for hours. I lost track of the time. I think my brain froze up or something. I thought maybe I'd come to town. But I didn't. So I just kept walking till I got here."

Josh raised his eyes to me. "That's the whole story. And it's the truth," he said softly. He glanced around the table, trying to see if everyone believed him.

"I—I can't believe Dara is dead," he added. "I can't believe someone murdered her. Murdered her and wrote that phony letter."

Those words gave me a chill.

I realized that I believed Josh. He seemed to be telling the truth.

He had acted crazily, thoughtlessly. But I believed him when he said he didn't kill Dara.

I swallowed hard. That meant only one thing. Someone *else* murdered Dara.

Someone in this room.

Gray light.

I woke up Sunday morning, bathed in cold gray light. It filtered through the thin white curtains over the bedroom window, making the room feel even colder than it was.

Stretching, I made my way sleepily across the room, pushed the curtains out of the way, and peered out. The heavy storm clouds still darkened the sky, hovering low over the trees. The snow still came down, tossed by the swirling winds.

The snow came down in sheets, so thick I could barely make out the pine trees that tilted down the sloping hill.

Am I ever going to get out of here? I wondered, shivering.

I got dressed quickly, pulling on black leggings and a heavy blue wool sweater. Making my way down the hall, I heard voices in the kitchen. The tangy aroma of bacon frying floated out and mixed with the smell of coffee.

"I can't face breakfast this morning," I murmured out loud. I turned away from the kitchen. I can't face any of them, either, I decided.

One of them is a murderer.

The words made my stomach tighten. The bacon smell suddenly made me feel ill.

A small, red phone on the hallway table caught my eye.

Had anyone called the police? Were they coming to get Josh?

Had anyone called to report the murder? To tell them we were stranded here? Stranded here with a frozen corpse in the garage?

I picked up the receiver and listened.

Still silent. Still dead.

I let out a disappointed groan. I can't spend another day in this house, I thought. It's a house of death. A house of horror.

I took a deep breath. "Get it together, April," I scolded myself.

"April—good morning!"

I turned to see Ken standing in the hallway. "Morning," I muttered.

"How are you doing?" he asked brightly. His brown hair was still wet from the shower. He carried a coffee mug in one hand. "Are you coming in for breakfast?"

"Uh . . . yes. I guess," I muttered.

I took a few steps toward the kitchen, but he moved to block my path. "Could I talk to you sometime this morning?" he asked, lowering his voice. His dark eyes locked on mine.

"Yeah. Sure," I replied, trying to sound casual. "What about?"

He hesitated. "Well, about something you said the other night."

The girl on Sumner Island.

That girl was the *last* thing I wanted to discuss with Ken. Every time I thought about her, I felt guilty. Guilty that I hadn't the nerve to tell Jenny about seeing Ken and that girl.

I certainly didn't want to discuss her with Ken. What could I say to him? That I thought he was a total rat?

"So? Can we talk?" he demanded.

"Maybe later," I told him.

Why had I blurted out that answer during the game? Why didn't I keep my big mouth shut?

The girl from Sumner Island floated through my mind again. Once more, I saw her and Ken, kissing on the beach, kissing so passionately.

Shaking the picture from my mind, I followed Ken into the kitchen. Tony and Carly were sitting glumly at the table. I didn't see Jenny or Josh. "Is this snow ever going to end?" Tony said, yawning.

"We've *got* to get out of here," Carly added, then finished a small glass of orange juice.

I silently agreed. I poured myself some orange juice. But it tasted sour. I buttered a slice of bread and choked it down. I really didn't feel like eating. And I didn't feel like being with these people.

"Where's Jenny?" I asked.

"Still asleep," Carly replied. "I think Josh is still asleep, too."

"Shouldn't we keep a close eye on him?" Tony asked.

"He isn't going anywhere," Ken replied, buttering a slice of toast. "He's trapped here like we are."

I turned and started out of the kitchen. "Where are you going?" Ken demanded.

"Just back to my room," I called back.

He said something, but I didn't wait to hear it. I wasn't feeling very social this morning. I hurried down the hall.

I stopped outside my door.

I heard noises inside the room. Footsteps. Drawers being opened and slammed.

My breath caught in my throat. Who was in my room?

Cautiously I gripped the doorframe and leaned forward, poking my head into the room.

And saw Josh, bent over the dresser, pulling out drawers, frantically searching through my things.

chapter

19

"Josh—what are you *doing?*" I screamed.

I really startled him. He cried out and stumbled back from the dresser.

"April, I . . . uh . . ."

I stormed into the room. "What were you looking for? What are you doing in here?" I shrieked. "Why are you tearing up my room?"

His slender face turned beet red. He pushed his glasses up on his nose. "I was looking for the pen," he finally managed to reply.

My mouth dropped open. "The pen?"

"The pen that wrote the letter to Dara. The red

ballpoint," he said. Standing awkwardly in the center of the room, he avoided my eyes.

"You admit that it was your pen?" I cried.

"No way!" he insisted heatedly. "I didn't write that letter, April. I—I want to find out who did. If I can find the pen that wrote it . . ." His voice trailed off.

"You think *I* wrote it?" I cried.

He didn't reply. I stood waiting, hands pressed against my waist. "Do you think I'm the one who wrote that letter?" I repeated.

"I don't know. I don't know you, do I?" he replied. His voice trembled with emotion. "I don't know *anything*. I just know that someone in this house wrote that letter. Not me. Someone else killed Dara."

"But, Josh—" I started.

"The pen has to be somewhere," he insisted. "And I'm going to search every room in the house until I find it. If I can find the pen, I can prove that I didn't write that note!"

"Well, you won't find it in *my* room!" I shrieked. "Get out! Get *out!*"

I knew I was totally losing it, but I didn't care.

I was trapped in this house, with a dead body in the garage—and possibly a murderer in my room!

"Get *out,* Josh!" I screamed. I grabbed him by both shoulders and shoved him hard toward the door.

He glared at me angrily. I felt a stab of fear.

But he turned and slunk out of the room.

"I can't take it anymore!" I shrieked out loud. I stared out the window. Still snowing. But not quite as hard.

I'm getting out, I told myself. I'm getting out of here. I don't care about the snow. I don't care about the cold. I don't care about *anything*.

I just have to get out. Get help.

Get home.

My heart was pounding. The gray light swirled around me. So heavy and cold.

I knew I wasn't thinking calmly, clearly. But I didn't care.

Finding Josh pawing through my clothes was the final straw.

I made my way silently down the hall, hoping the others wouldn't hear me, hoping no one would come out of the kitchen.

My boots were near the front door. I sat down on the floor and pulled them over my leggings. Then I stood up and walked over to the pile of coats.

We had all just tossed our coats down when we came in. And we had all been wearing each other's coats. So they were totally jumbled. I pulled up each coat, one by one.

"Weird," I muttered. My parka wasn't in the pile.

I searched through the pile again, more carefully this time. Then I searched through the coat closet. Not there, either.

Had I hung the parka in my bedroom closet?

I hurried back down the hall and made a complete search of the bedroom. No parka.

I stopped in the center of the room to think. Where had I put it? Did I take it into one of the other rooms?

No. The last I remembered, I had dropped it on the pile of coats near the front door.

It should be here, I thought. My parka should be here on the pile.

Where is it? Where?

I shuffled frantically through the coats again, tossing them wildly aside as I searched.

Not here. Not here. Not here.

And then a picture flashed into my mind. A horrifying picture.

A picture that made my entire body tremble in shock.

chapter

20

The picture was a horrifying image of Dara's frozen body.

Outside on the back porch.

Dara's frozen corpse. Lying stiffly in the snow. Her eyes frozen wide in shock and horror.

The hatchet buried deep in her shoulders.

Buried deep in a blue parka.

My blue parka?

Was it my blue parka? Had Dara been wearing my coat on Friday night?

With a gasp I hurtled to the front door. I didn't even think of pulling on a coat. I didn't think at all. The picture in my mind forced away all other thoughts.

I burst out into the snow. My boots sank into a deep

drift. I raised my knees high, made my way to the garage.

Another step. Then another. Breathing hard, my breath steaming up above me. The snow in my face, in my eyes. Pushing me back, as if trying to keep me from my destination.

I bent to lift the garage door. The handle was covered with icy snow. The frozen door didn't want to open.

I tugged with both hands and finally got it to slide.

The door rumbled up. I stepped inside, brushing snow from my eyes.

I stared into the darkness. Stared down at Dara.

They had propped her against the wall, next to an old bicycle. Her eyes—wide open—had sunk back into her head. They stared out at me accusingly.

I swallowed hard. Forced myself to lower my gaze from her frozen face.

Struggled to focus on the parka she wore.

Yes. My parka.

Dara wore my blue parka.

Dara wore my parka Friday night when she was murdered.

The hatchet had sliced through the shoulder of *my* parka.

And as I gaped at the corpse in horror, another picture forced itself into my mind. I pictured myself out in the snow. I pictured myself late Friday night in the dark, walking to the woodshed.

Because with the hood of my blue parka pulled up, Dara would have looked just like me.

Me . . .

And I pictured myself stiff and frozen. And dead.

Standing at the open garage door, staring down at the frozen, blue-faced corpse, the cold lowered over me.

Cold and darkness. Darkness I could feel.

And I knew that Dara had died by mistake.

It was *me* lying there. *Me.*

The murderer had meant to kill *me.*

chapter
21

With a low cry I stumbled out of the garage and made my way through the snow back into the house. *"My coat—"* The words tumbled from my mouth as I pulled the front door closed behind me.

What to do? What to do?

Someone had tried to kill me.

Was it Josh? Was it one of the others?

I didn't want to think about it. I was too crazed to think clearly about anything.

Maybe I can get help, I told myself, trying to stop my body from trembling. Maybe I can get to the road. Get to a ski lodge. Find someone. Find *anyone* who can get me to the police.

I grabbed a coat off the pile. A big, red down coat. I didn't know whose. I didn't care.

Pulling the coat over my shoulders, I jerked open the front door and darted back outside.

My boots sank into the deep, powdery snow as I trudged to the driveway. The wind had driven the snow into deep drifts. The snow that fell now was wet and icy, more like sleet than snow.

I glanced back at the house. Had anyone seen me leave? Was anyone following me?

No. No one in the window.

I'm getting away, I thought.

It was colder than I'd thought. The cold stung my face and made my nostrils burn when I inhaled. Struggling to zip the bulky coat, I lurched down the hill.

The wind seemed to be blowing right in my face. I leaned into it and shut my eyes against the wet, falling snow.

"I'm out!" I cried out loud, my voice muffled in the wind. "I'm out of there!"

I can make it, I told myself. I can make it to the nearest ski lodge.

I squinted to the bottom of the hill. I could barely make out the snow-covered road. The plows had left long mounds of snow that trailed along the sides. But more snow had covered the pavement in a deep blanket of white.

I leaned into the stiff wind, shielding my eyes from the blowing snow and the bright, silvery glare. I finally managed to zip the coat. But it was too big. As I walked, the wind swirled up the front of it and down the collar.

This must be Ken's coat, I realized. Ken is the biggest person in the house.

Yes. I could picture Ken in the coat. Picture him with his heavy red sleeve around Jenny's shoulders. Picture him running to catch the Shadyside bus after school, the red coat flapping behind him like a big flag.

And then I pictured him once again with the girl on Sumner Island last summer. I pictured them laughing together. Snuggling. Kissing on the beach.

I had been so shocked, I nearly ran over to them and pulled them apart. I nearly confronted Ken right there and then.

I was so horrified. And so furious at him.

What would have happened if I *had* run onto the beach and let Ken know that I was there? What would he have done? What would have happened between Ken and Jenny?

I cried out as my boots sank into a deep snowdrift, and I toppled forward. My hands shot out—too late. I landed hard, sank into the white cold.

I scrambled up quickly and brushed myself off.

Keep moving, I urged myself. *Don't stop. You can't stop until you find someone.*

My cheeks burned. The cold made my temples throb with pain. I touched my nose. It was already numb.

Frostbite.

The word made me gasp.

I rubbed my ears. Also numb.

I'm not going to make it, I thought.

I was still a long way from the road. Not a car or truck had passed by. There was no one out in this storm.

Only me.

Keep going, April, I urged myself again. *Don't give up. You can do it. You can find someone to help you.*

You don't want to go back to that house.

There's a murderer back there. A murderer waiting for you.

Unable to stop my entire body from shivering, I shoved my hands into the deep pockets of Ken's coat.

Why hadn't I stopped to find some gloves? Or a hat? Or a scarf?

I was so stupid, so crazy, so desperate to get away.

But now the wind was whipping the snow in my face, pushing me back as I tried to get down the hill. The cold forced my eyes to tear up. My chest ached. My breath steamed up as I panted hard, breathing through my mouth.

I dug my hands deeper into the coat pockets.

And my right hand wrapped around something.

A thin object. Metal or plastic.

I pulled it out and raised it close to my face to examine it.

A pen. A ballpoint pen.

A red plastic ballpoint pen.

I checked the tip. Red.

Red ink.

I stopped walking. I stared at the pen in horror.

I no longer cared about the wind, the cold, the blowing snow. I no longer noticed them.

I knew what I was holding.

The pen that had written the letter to Dara.

chapter

22

I started to shiver again. The pen blurred in front of my eyes.

My hand began trembling so hard, I nearly dropped it into the snow. Gripping it tightly, I shoved it back into the coat pocket.

The wind swirled the snow around me. I rubbed my nose, trying to rub some feeling back into it. Then I pulled my hair down over my ears to protect them, tucking the hair into the coat collar.

The murderer wasn't Josh, I realized.

The murderer was Ken.

I tried to picture what had happened. I pictured Ken following Dara out into the snow, sneaking up behind her, bringing the hatchet down . . . down . . .

Thinking it was me.

And why? Because of my Truth or Dare answer? Because I knew about Ken and the girl from last summer?

And when he realized he had killed Dara instead of me, he wrote the letter. To blame Josh.

I turned back toward the top of the hill. Stopped. Turned away again.

I suddenly felt like one of the tiny snowflakes being tossed and twirled by the wind. I felt helpless as a snowflake. Helpless and fragile.

I gazed down at the snowy road. The road led to another hill, a steeper hill with the ski lift that led up to the slopes. And a short distance beyond that hill, there were ski lodges and motels. And then the town.

It all seemed so far away. So impossibly far away.

Leaning into the wind, I started walking anyway. What choice did I have?

"Oh!" I cried out as I stepped into a deep drift and the snow rose up over my boot tops. I could feel the frozen, wet snow pour into the boots.

I was nearly to the bottom of the hill when I heard crunching sounds behind me.

I ignored them at first. But they grew louder.

And then I heard low grunts. Someone breathing hard.

I turned back. Stared up the hill, squinting into the shifting, blowing snow.

And saw someone chasing after me. Running hard.

A dark figure, his face hidden in the gray.

Who is it? Who? I wondered.

His grunting breaths grew louder. He was running so hard, so fast, his arms outstretched as if reaching to grab me.

So eager to catch up with me. To catch me.

I froze in fear, watching, squinting into the billowing snow, the shimmering, gray light, struggling to see.

By the time I realized it was Ken, it was too late.

I turned and started to run, slipping and sliding down the frozen hill.

I screamed as I felt his arms wrap roughly around my waist.

He tackled me from behind. Pulled me down. Down into the deep snow.

"Ken—let me go!" I begged. "Please—let me go!"

*K*en pinned me to the snow.

I swung out wildly, trying to push him off. With a loud cry I rolled out of his grasp.

"Hey—!" he cried angrily.

Gasping for breath, I scrambled to my feet. I was covered in snow. I could feel it in my hair, down the back of my neck.

"April—what's your problem?" Ken cried. He raised himself to his knees.

"Don't touch me!" I shrieked, backing away, struggling to catch my breath.

My temples throbbed. I could feel cold snow packed inside my boots. "Why did you f-follow me?" I choked out.

"To bring you back," he replied, staying on his knees. He had a black ski parka pulled down over black denim jeans.

I've got to get away from him! I told myself, taking another step back.

If I don't get away, he'll kill me right here.

"Didn't you see me?" he asked. "Why did you run away, April?"

"What do you want?" I demanded, ignoring his questions. "I—I—" I didn't know what to say.

"It's too cold," he said, climbing to his feet. "Are you trying to walk to town? You'll never make it. You'll get really bad frostbite."

"Listen, Ken—" I started. I wanted to tell him I knew the truth. I wanted to tell him I found the pen. I knew he had written the letter to make us think Josh was the murderer. I knew he had murdered Dara, thinking she was me.

But I was too terrified.

I glanced down to the bottom of the hill and let my eyes follow the road. No one in sight. No one around for miles.

I was all alone here. With a murderer.

"You took my coat," he said quietly, calmly, his eyes burning into mine.

"I—I was going to give it back," I stammered.

He sighed impatiently. "April, I'm not worried about the old coat. I'm worried about you. It's not very warm. It's big and heavy, but it's not very warm."

"Did you come all the way after me to tell me that?" I asked, stalling for time.

I've got to keep him talking, I told myself. Until someone drives by. Or until I can think of a way to escape from him.

"Hey, it wasn't *my* idea to run after you," Ken muttered. "It was Jenny's."

"Jenny's?" I studied his face. I could tell he was lying. He was a terrible liar. I could see the tension lines around his mouth.

"Jenny was really worried about you," he continued. "She made me run out and get you. She was afraid you wouldn't realize how dangerous it is out here."

Liar!

Did he really think I was that stupid?

"Is the phone fixed at the house?" I demanded.

He shook his head. "Not yet."

I brushed snow from my hair with one hand. My hair was soaked. Icy water ran down the back of my neck. "Then we have to keep going," I insisted. "We have to get the police."

"We can't make it!" Ken shouted impatiently. "We'll freeze." He took a step toward me. "Tony is keeping a close watch on Josh. Josh won't try anything."

But Josh isn't the murderer!

That's what I wanted to scream at Ken. But I was too frightened.

I could feel the pen in the coat pocket. I squeezed it tightly in my hand.

I wanted to pull it out and stick it in front of his face.

I wanted to say, "Here's your ballpoint, Ken. The one you wrote the phony letter with."

But *then* what would he do? I asked myself. *Then* what would he do to me?

There was no one around. No one. Just miles and miles of deep snow.

He could bury me, I thought with a shudder. He could bury me in the snow and no one will find my body till spring.

"Come on. Let's go back," he snapped. He took two quick steps toward me and grabbed my arm. "I'm freezing, too."

What is he going to do? What is he going to do? The question repeated in my mind.

I tucked my hair back into the coat collar and started to follow him back up the hill. I pressed my hand against my face. My nose and cheeks were totally numb.

I have no choice, I decided. I'll go back to the house with him. I can't make it dressed like this.

I'll play along, I decided. As soon as I get back, I'll pull on warmer clothes. Then I'll sneak out again.

Ken thinks his secret is safe, I told myself. He has no idea that I know the truth—that he killed Dara. That he tried to kill *me!*

I'll play along. I'll let him take me back to the house. Then I'll warn Jenny. I'll tell her that Ken is a murderer. And the two of us will escape together.

The idea gave me new hope.

I can't run away and leave Jenny there with Ken, I decided. I already had let Jenny down by not telling her about the girl on Sumner Island.

This time, I'll do the right thing, I told myself. This time I'll act like a true friend.

I stepped up beside him and we started to walk together, our boots sinking into the soft, powdery snow. "Why'd you tackle me?" I asked, trying to make it sound light.

"I didn't mean to. I was running too hard and I fell into you," Ken said, but I knew he was lying. He turned to me with false concern on his face. "I didn't hurt you—did I?"

You tried to kill me Friday night! I thought.

"No." I shook my head. "You scared me, that's all."

He stopped. His eyes grew cold as they locked onto mine. "I want to talk to you," he said softly. "About the other night."

Uh-oh, I thought.

I didn't say anything. So Ken continued. "That answer you gave in the Truth or Dare game. I really don't think you know—"

"Oh, Ken—I saw you last summer!" The words burst out of my mouth before I could stop them. I had held the horrible secret in for so long.

He didn't seem at all surprised. His face remained a total blank.

"I saw you and that girl on the beach. I don't know her name or anything. But I saw you. I saw you kissing her, and I—"

His face remained blank. Stone cold, like a statue.

He grabbed my arm. "Did you tell Jenny? Did you tell Jenny about her?"

"No!" I cried, frightened. Frightened by his grasp, by his cold, cold stare. "No, Ken. I never told her."

He brought his face close to mine, staring hard into my eyes as if searching for the truth in them.

"I wanted to tell her," I confessed. "Several times I almost told her. But I—I never did."

His face finally changed. His features twisted into a hard sneer. "And you knew about it all this time?" he demanded.

I nodded, my heart pounding. "Yes," I whispered. "Yes. I saw you with her, Ken. I saw you last summer."

His hand tightened its grip on my arm. He moved closer, his eyes still burning into mine.

"I'm so sorry, April," he murmured. "I'm so sorry."

chapter
24

I tugged myself free. "Ken—!" I started. But my voice choked in my throat.

My heart thudding, I spun away from him and started back up the hill. I expected him to grab me, to try to stop me.

But he didn't. He followed close behind, walking in my bootprints. I glanced back to see a thoughtful, solemn expression on his face.

I was so intent on getting back up to the house, I hadn't noticed that the snow had finally stopped falling. The glare of bright sunshine off the snow made me realize that the dark clouds had finally parted.

Good! I thought. This will make it easier to get away. This will make it easier for Jenny and me to get help.

Ken didn't say a word until we reached the house and stepped through the front door. The bright white glare of sunlight on the snow followed me into the house. I blinked several times, trying to force my eyes to adjust.

I tossed off Ken's coat and dropped it onto the pile. "Where is everyone?" I asked.

"April—you and I have to talk," Ken said in a hushed voice. He reached for me, and my entire body shuddered.

"Later!" I cried. "Please, Ken—I've got to get something warm to drink!"

"But, April—" I heard Ken call.

"Hey, Ken—you're back!" Tony burst into the room. "Come help me get firewood, man. The furnace went off. It's getting cold in here."

Ken started to protest. But Tony dragged him away.

Gratefully I hurried away to search for Jenny. I found her with Carly in front of the living room window. "I need to talk to you," I told her. "In private."

Carly's eyes narrowed suspiciously. But I dragged Jenny into the kitchen.

"April—what's up?" she demanded, her blue eyes revealing her confusion. "What's wrong?"

"Everything is wrong," I whispered. "Everything."

"Huh?" She reached out and pushed my wet hair off my forehead. "April, where did you go? I was so worried about you. Look at your face. You're bright red! You must be frozen!"

"Don't worry about my face," I said sharply. "I have a lot to tell you about, Jenny." A frightened sob escaped my throat. "I—I should have told you a long time ago. I've known it for months and—"

She held her hand over my mouth. "Shhh. We can't talk here, April," she whispered.

"We can't stay here," I told her, pulling her hand away. "We're not safe. We've got to get away from here. I have to tell you about Ken, Jenny. He—"

Carly poked her head into the kitchen. "Secrets?" she asked.

"Yes. Secrets," Jenny replied quickly. "Deep, dark secrets."

"Hope you're not talking about *me,*" Carly replied dryly. She took a can of Coke from the refrigerator, then returned to the living room.

"The snow has stopped. Maybe we can *ski* away from here," I suggested as soon as Carly was out of the room.

Jenny gaped at me. "Ski?"

"We have to get out of here, Jenny," I repeated. "I have so much to tell you. I—I know everything!"

Her expression changed. "Okay. Let's go," she replied in a low voice. "The skis are out back. Let's get changed and get away from here—before Tony and Ken come back with their firewood."

125

We hurried side by side down the hall to our rooms. As I turned into my room, I was practically bursting with excitement.

Can we get out of here before Ken comes back? I wondered.

Can we really get away from him?

chapter

25

I quickly pulled on layers of clothes. Two sweaters. Thermal underwear under my ski pants.

I met Jenny by the front door. She had tucked her brown hair under a woolen ski band. She wore a heavy orange sweater over white ski pants.

Checking to make sure the coast was clear, Jenny and I made our way to the back porch to get our skis and poles from the ski locker.

I shuddered, thinking about Dara's frozen body, lying so near us in the garage.

"The road will be open now. Cars will be moving. We'll find someone to help us," I promised Jenny. "We'll find someone to help us get the town police."

She nodded, adjusting her skis.

"Let's go," I urged, tugging her arm.

I leaned forward on my ski poles and pushed. The snow was deep and soft. The skis slid easily over the slick surface.

I led the way to the front of the house. Then I pressed forward and started to ski down the sloping hill.

Jenny moved awkwardly at first, then smoothed out her strokes. We were skiing side by side.

Did I hear a shout? Was that Ken calling after us?

I glanced at Jenny. I couldn't tell if she heard Ken's cries or not.

We kept skiing. We didn't turn back.

The gleaming white snow seemed to swallow me up. The gentle *sshh sshh sshh* of the skis rose up, soft and soothing. I bent my knees, leaned back, picked up speed.

Moving through this glowing, white world, I tried to lose myself. Tried to forget about Ken, about Dara, about the girl on Sumner Island.

But I couldn't ski away from my dark thoughts. Even the glistening snow and the sparkle of golden sunlight off its pure, clean surface couldn't help me forget.

Sshh sshh sshh. The skis whispered up at me as I slid down the hill. Through the woods.

The silence all around made my thoughts so much louder, so much more frightening. The sharp, cold air burned my face and made my eyes tear up.

Was I crying? Was that me sobbing so silently as I skied?

"April—what *is* it?" Jenny cried breathlessly as we slid to a stop at the bottom of the next slope.

I gasped in breath after breath, struggling to get myself in control.

We've escaped, I told myself. Jenny and I have escaped from that frightening house, escaped from Ken.

I'm never going back there, I told myself.

"April—are you okay?" Jenny's shrill voice cut through my thoughts. Her cheeks were pink. Her blue eyes caught the bright sunlight as she edged beside me, staring at me with concern.

I nodded. "I'll be okay," I told her in a shaky voice. "I'm okay—now that you and I are away."

We both gazed up at the white, sloping hill. To our surprise, the ski lift started moving at that instant. The wooden benches, white against the white snow, bobbed and swayed, empty as the overhead cable carried them to the top.

"Look! It just started up!" I cried.

"Where is everyone?" Jenny demanded, shielding her eyes to follow the benches to the top. "There's no one here."

"I guess the blizzard kept the skiers away," I replied, glancing all around. "But the ski patrol guys should be here—shouldn't they?"

I gazed toward the ski lift. "Yes!" I answered my own question. I could see a man in a blue ski outfit at the bottom of the lift.

Finally! Someone who could help us.

Leaning on the ski poles, my skis sinking into the

deep snow, I led the way up to the man. "We need help!" I cried. "How can we contact the town police?"

He was an old man. He stood hunched against the cold, his blue hood tied tightly, revealing only a small portion of his face. He stared back at me without replying. I wasn't sure if he heard me or not.

"We need the police!" I repeated shrilly.

He nodded, then pointed to the top of the slope. "There's a ski patrol station up top," he told us. "They've got a phone up there."

We thanked him and eagerly made our way to the chairlift.

"I always think the hardest part is getting on these things," Jenny admitted. "They seem to be going so fast when you get up close to them."

A gust of wind made the empty benches swing back and forth. I raised my eyes to the top of the slope. The benches bobbed up the hill like an eerie, silent parade.

Like a parade of ghosts.

Tucking our ski poles under our arms, we moved in front of a moving bench, turned, and dropped onto the seat.

"Made it," she said softly. She reached up and pulled down the safety bar.

The bench swayed under our weight. The cable creaked above us. I slid against the back of the bench, pressing against it.

I gazed to the side as we started to rise up.

The glittering snow seemed to stretch on forever. It didn't look like anything I had ever seen before.

Higher. Higher. The cable creaking and swaying in the wind. The snow sparkling far below us now.

We were about a third of the way up the hill when Jenny turned to me. Her chin quivered and her mouth twisted into an ugly sneer.

"I'm really sorry, April," she said in a strained, tense voice.

"What do you mean?" I didn't understand at first.

"I'm really sorry," she repeated. "But what choice do I have?"

Before I could reply, Jenny pushed up the safety bar.

Then she brought both hands up behind me—and shoved with all her strength.

chapter

26

"Nooooo!"

A scream escaped my throat as I felt myself falling off the bench.

I thrust out my hand and grabbed the side. The cable groaned. The bench swayed and tossed beneath me.

With an angry groan, Jenny shoved again.

But I dodged against the side—and the force of her shove nearly sent her toppling off.

I swung around, grabbed her by the shoulders. "Jenny—what are you doing?" The words burst out in a terrified shriek. "Why? Why?"

She struggled to twist out of my grasp. The car swayed hard, nearly spilling us both.

"Let go! Let go!" she shrieked as we wrestled.

I glanced down. The ground stretched so far below. So far.

Even the deep snow won't cushion my fall, I thought.

I let out a gasp. In my mind I pictured myself falling, falling through the clear, cold air. I heard the *thud* as I landed. Heard the *crack* of my bones.

Saw myself sprawled in the snow. A puddle of red spreading out from my broken body, spreading over the white, white ground.

"No!"

The picture made me struggle harder.

The car swayed and tilted as Jenny and I wrestled, crying and groaning as we fought.

"Why, Jenny?" I demanded again and again. "Why?"

"Because of the girl on Sumner Island!" Jenny screamed. "Because you know about her, April!"

"Huh?"

The shock of Jenny's answer made me freeze.

Jenny stopped her desperate struggles to push me off. "You know about the girl!" she shrieked in a trembling, shrill voice.

"But, Jenny—" I started to protest.

She didn't let me finish. "I caught the clue, April," she told me, her blue eyes burning into mine. "During the Truth or Dare game. It was a signal to me—wasn't it!"

"Huh? A signal to you?" I cried, totally startled and confused. "No, Jenny. No! It was a signal to—"

"I caught your signal, April!" Jenny cried, ignoring me.

She raised her hands to my shoulders, gripped me tightly, but didn't push. "You were letting me know you knew about the girl—weren't you!"

I started to reply. But Jenny didn't give me a chance.

"You were telling me you knew!" she insisted. "Well, I didn't mean to kill that girl, April! I didn't mean to! It was an accident!"

chapter
27

*T*he cable creaked above our heads, the only sound as I stared at Jenny in shock and horror. The ski lift carried us higher, the bench swaying as we climbed.

But all motion stopped for me.

I felt frozen in place, like a cold statue. The sky above our heads, the shimmering snow beneath us— all faded into a frigid gray blur.

I realized I was holding my breath. I forced myself to breathe. My heart thudded in my chest.

"So how long have you known the whole story?" Jenny demanded. Her brown hair flew behind her. Her blue eyes pierced into mine.

"The whole story?" I stared at her, unable to think clearly.

I must be in shock or something, I thought. Did I really hear Jenny say she *killed* that girl?

"Ken wouldn't stop seeing her," Jenny said, her normally pretty face ugly with bitterness and anger. "If only he had stopped seeing her."

"You mean—after the summer?" I managed to choke out.

Jenny didn't seem to hear me. Her eyes gazed straight ahead now, unfocused. "Barbara," she murmured through clenched teeth. "That was her name. Barbara. She lived in Foster Mills."

I stared hard at Jenny. She's talking to herself, I realized. Jenny seems to have forgotten that I'm here.

"Barbara. Barbara." She repeated the name, her expression hard, bitter.

"Listen, Jenny—" I started.

But she didn't hear me. She was lost in her anger, lost in her bitter memories.

"Oh, I knew about Barbara," Jenny uttered in a strained, tight voice I'd never heard before. "I knew about Ken and Barbara. He promised me it was over. He promised me. He swore that he said good-bye to her on Sumner Island."

Her chin quivered. Her blue eyes seemed to dim, to lose their color, their life. *"Liar!"* she screamed furiously. *"Liar!"*

The car rocked as we headed up to the high slope. Jenny reached up and tugged her hair down, tucking it with frantic motions into her parka collar.

"But Ken kept seeing her," she continued, her eyes on the snow-covered hill in front of us. "Ken kept disappearing to Foster Mills to see Barbara. So . . . I went to see her, too."

All this time I've been keeping the secret from her, I thought, shaking my head. *And Jenny knew about it all along.*

"I saw Barbara," Jenny continued, her voice trembling with emotion. "I tried to talk to her. I—I don't know what happened. I just went there to see her, to talk to her."

Higher, we climbed. Higher. The bench swaying as it made its way to the top of the deserted, white slope.

"She was kind of pretty," Jenny murmured thoughtfully, still staring straight ahead. "Kind of pretty if you like that type. You know. Tanned skin. Short black hair. Perfect little face. Perfect little body. Perfect bangs. Neat and perfect."

Jenny's lips twisted into an odd, bitter smile.

The smile faded quickly. "I don't know what happened," Jenny revealed. "I really don't know what happened. I guess I went crazy or something. I just went crazy."

She *is* crazy, I thought, studying her. Jenny *is* crazy.

And I'm trapped up here beside her.

What is she going to do when she finishes her story? I asked myself. Is she going to try to wrestle me off the ski lift again?

Is she going to try to kill me again?

"It was an accident!" she cried, still avoiding my

eyes. "It *had* to be an accident. But she was dead. Barbara was dead. We fought. And I killed her."

Jenny sighed. "I saw her perfect green eyes roll up. I saw the blood seep from her scalp and spread through her perfect black hair. I killed her. I'm not even sure how. But I killed her."

And now Jenny turned to me, her eyes so cold, brimming with hate. "I was so scared, April. So totally scared. I ran from Barbara's house. I hurried home. I was going to call you. I was going to ask you what to do."

She let out a long sigh. "But I was too scared. I kept my secret. I never told a soul."

She gripped the sleeve of my coat. "Do you know what it's like to live in such fear? Do you know what it's like to be afraid every moment of your life?"

I gasped. I didn't know how to reply. I felt so bad for Jenny—and so terrified of her at the same time.

"I never took a normal breath," she continued, her voice breaking. "After that horrible day, I never took a normal breath. Never took a step. Never had a single moment when I didn't think about what I had done. When I didn't worry about getting caught."

A choked sob escaped her throat. "The police never solved it. They never even came close. But that didn't make me feel better. That didn't make me breathe any easier."

Jenny gripped my arm tighter. "The fear didn't go away, April. Even when the police closed their investigation. Even when they admitted defeat. When

Barbara's murder went unsolved. The fear didn't leave me.

"I had one constant fear," Jenny continued heatedly. "The fear that someone would find out. The fear that someone knew the truth."

Her eyes narrowed as she locked them on mine. "And then Friday night my worst nightmare came true. My worst nightmare. During the Truth or Dare game. You! You revealed that you knew about Barbara. You said it so casually, April. So calmly."

"But—but, Jenny—" I sputtered.

She gripped me with both hands. The bench rocked forward, then back.

"My worst nightmare had come true!" Jenny cried. "Something inside me snapped. The secret had been kept for so long. I couldn't let you ruin everything now! So I—so I—"

"So you killed Dara!" I blurted out, suddenly finding my voice.

"I thought it was you!" Jenny screamed. "It was so dark outside. I saw your parka. I recognized it. I had no choice. You knew my secret. I had no choice!"

"But you killed Dara!" I repeated, so frightened I didn't know *what* I was saying. "You killed Dara, Jenny!"

"It was another accident," she protested. "Another accident. I hardly knew Dara! You made me kill again, April! This time it was your fault. You made me!"

She's crazy! I realized. *Jenny is totally crazy!*

"You—you wrote the letter to Dara and signed Josh's name?" I stammered.

139

She nodded.

"You hid the red pen in Ken's coat pocket?"

She nodded again. "I knew it was safe there. Ken would never tell anyone about it."

"Does Ken know?" I asked. "Does Ken know that you killed Barbara?"

"No one knows!" Jenny shrieked. "Only you, April!"

"But, Jenny—" I started.

She shook me hard. "How did you find out my secret?" she demanded, her eyes wild, her features distorted in fury. "Tell me! How did you find out about Barbara? How did you know that I killed her?"

"I—I didn't!" I stammered. "Jenny—really! I didn't know!"

Her eyes were wild. I don't even think she heard me.

I screamed at her again, trying to make her hear. "Jenny—listen to me! I didn't know! I didn't know!"

She didn't hear.

Her mouth opened wide in a furious, animal cry.

She shoved me hard with both hands.

And I went sailing off the bench. Into the air.

chapter
28

I had no time to scream.

My hands flailed wildly out to my sides. Grabbing nothing but air. The ski poles flew out of my hands.

I dropped facedown into the snow.

Dead.

The word thudded heavily into my mind as darkness swept over me.

With a shudder I waited to feel the pain.

The cold invaded my clothes, spread over my face.

Whoa! I thought. There's something wrong. . . .

Where is the pain?

The fall had been so fast. The landing so quick and soft.

I raised my head—and realized I hadn't fallen far at all.

The ski lift had reached the top of the hill. I had toppled only a few feet to the ground.

My heart pounding, I raised myself to my knees. My skis had unsnapped when I hit the ground. I brushed the snow from my face with both hands.

I turned in time to see Jenny leap off the ski lift bench. She landed heavily, her skis sinking into the soft snow.

"Jenny—!" I cried.

She didn't give me time to climb to my feet.

Her face wild with fury, she slid toward me. Raised her ski pole. And thrust it at my throat.

chapter

29

I spun away.

The pole pierced the snow a few inches from my face.

With a low groan I struggled to my feet. "Jenny—drop it!" I cried. "Jenny—please!"

But she jabbed with the pole again, sliding awkwardly on her skis.

I stumbled backward.

The pole glanced off the shoulder of my coat.

With a desperate cry Jenny swung the pole like a baseball bat. Swung it again. Wild, frantic swings, slicing the air.

The benches rattled behind us, one after the other,

rising to the hilltop, then starting their trip back down.

As Jenny swung the ski pole, my fear quickly gave way to anger. "Jenny—stop!" I shouted. "Drop the pole! Stop it!"

I took a step toward her, raising both arms to shield myself.

"No!" she screamed. "No! Get back!"

I took another step toward her. "Drop the pole."

She backed up, panting like a wild animal.

"April—I have no choice!" Jenny shrieked. "Don't you see? I have no choice!"

Ignoring her threat, I moved steadily toward her.

She backed up. One step back. Then another. Another.

"Jenny, it'll be okay," I said, trying to keep my voice low and soothing. "It'll be okay. We'll get you help."

"I have no choice," she repeated, eyeing me coldly. "I really have no choice."

She wasn't listening. She couldn't hear me.

I moved toward her. "Jenny—please listen to me. Let's go back to the house. We'll get you help. You'll be okay."

"No. No. No." She repeated the word like a chant.

Her eyes darting wildly back and forth, she stepped back. Back.

The moving bench caught her in the back of the head.

She opened her mouth in a silent cry of surprise.

Stunned, she staggered forward. Raised her hands to her head.

I wasted no time. I leaped forward. Grabbed her around the waist and pulled her to the snowy ground.

"My head . . ." she murmured. And then she added, "My secret. You cannot know my secret."

A shadow swept over us.

Startled, I glanced up—in time to see Ken leap off the ski lift.

"Ken!" I screamed happily. "You followed us! How did you know?"

He didn't reply. Instead, he moved quickly to help me pull Jenny to her feet.

"Don't try to get away," Ken told Jenny. "Just come back to the house with us. We'll take good care of you. Until the police come."

Jenny nodded. Dazed. Defeated. "My secret," she murmured. "You don't know my secret."

"Ken—I thought you didn't know!" I blurted out. "How did you—?"

"I found the red pen in my coat pocket," Ken replied. "I was so puzzled. I didn't know how it got there. It made me think about the letter, the letter we found in Dara's room. I took a close look at it. I recognized Jenny's handwriting."

Over his shoulder I saw two blue-uniformed ski patrolmen hurrying toward us.

Ken grabbed my arm. "I was totally confused. I didn't understand at all. I called to you. I tried to stop you from leaving with Jenny. But I guess you didn't hear me."

His voice caught in his throat. "I knew that Jenny wrote that letter. It had me so upset, I thought I'd better follow you. Does—does this mean that Jenny killed Dara?"

I nodded. "She thought Dara was me," I murmured.

"Huh?" Ken's mouth dropped open.

"No one knows my secret," Jenny mumbled to herself. "No one knows it."

The two ski patrolmen were nearly up to us. The frightening weekend was nearly over.

"The Truth or Dare game," I told Ken sadly. "It revealed more *truth* than any of us realized."

He narrowed his eyes, thinking about it for a long moment. "Next time, April, take the dare," he advised.

"Next time," I told him, "maybe we should stick to Trivial Pursuit."

About the Author

"Where do you get your ideas?"

That's the question that R. L. Stine is asked most often. "I don't know where my ideas come from," he says. "But I do know that I have a lot more scary stories in my mind that I can't wait to write."

So far, he has written more than fifty mysteries and thrillers for young people, all of them bestsellers.

Bob grew up in Columbus, Ohio. Today he lives in an apartment near Central Park in New York City with his wife, Jane, and fourteen-year-old son, Matt.

WATCH OUT FOR

FEAR STREET®

DEAD END

All Natalie and her friends wanted was a safe ride home from the party. But now they share a terrible secret. They were all in the car that foggy night—that night someone died at the dead end.

They all make a vow never to tell. Then someone's conscience burns—and another accident happens. Natalie just wants out of this nightmare! But that's the problem with dead ends . . . there's no way out!